HOTEL TOLEDO

&

BEHIND THE MASK

A NOVEL IN TWO PARTS

Melinda B Hipple

QUITAB EDITIONS

Cover art: © Melinda B Hipple
Design & layout: Steven Asmussen

Quitab Editions: an imprint of
Glass Lyre Press, LLC
P.O. Box 2693
Glenview, IL 60025

www.GlassLyrePress.com

HOTEL TOLEDO

&

BEHIND THE MASK

A NOVEL IN TWO PARTS

Other books by Melinda B Hipple

Science Fiction:
Raven

Historical Non-fiction:
Home Front

Poetry:
Camera Obscura
in a bottle of ink
The Leading Trees

Children's Books:
Ant Trails
Who Lives on the Moon?

HOTEL
TOLEDO
BOOK ONE

To Jo (Zoe), my first Toledo friend.
She is missed.

Chapter One

I was born a coward—a fact that, until recently, I had managed to keep quite confidential. This trait has now moved from surreptitious burden to public brand. If I had opened my door just once to allow Dottie inside my boundaries, perhaps she would still be my neighbor. Of course, I can't be sure of that.

From time to time, I would hear the unnerving rattle of someone testing my door. Dottie, pressing her fingers against the knob. I suspected it was Dottie. I never suspected she was trying to break in. She was lonely. The type of lonely that befalls elderly people who have outlived siblings, cousins, friends. She rarely complained. Her feet shuffled down the hall several times a day as she wandered past my apartment door. Quietly, I ignored her curiosity and stuffed a modicum of guilt for my antisocial behavior. When I saw her sitting in a spot of sunshine on the lobby sofa, I would stop and chat. Once or twice a week, I could spare some minutes for a pleasant exchange of useless information. Nevertheless, behind my own hollow-core door—a paper-thin travesty that vibrated the comings and goings of everyone in the hotel and kept out nothing but prying eyes—I wanted anonymity. I guarded my tiny living space with the ferocity of a wounded pit bull. I was afraid of these people. More than that, I feared what it said about me that I lived among these people. I should have opened the door.

It was March, and Sidney lay beside me on the sofa. He raised his eyes toward the ceiling but kept his muzzle resting on his paws. Together we listened to the dainty footsteps pacing the floor above. A door opened. A voice rose in anger. Marty was home, and Kristine must have forgotten to do something trivial again.

"Good boy," I praised Sidney when he did not growl. "You ignore them better than I do."

Dottie's phone rang. It echoed down the hallway from her half-open door to the marble-floored lobby at the far end of the building. I counted. One ring. Two rings. Dottie's heavy footsteps thumped in the distance. Three rings. She stumbled closer, and I imagined her frail hands testing the walls as she hurried toward her apartment. Four rings. Her orthopedic shoes tromped past my door and kicked her own, slamming it open the rest of the way. At ninety-five, she was surprisingly quick on her feet. Five rings. "Hello?" I tuned out the words.

Amid Dottie's louder-than-necessary half of a conversation and the accusations and apologies raging overhead, I heard the sweet and simple sound of a music box. It was brief. Something on the television? The news anchor's somber tone from behind his desk assured me it was not. The nightly newsman. Dottie. Kristine. Marty. Their voices blended into the jumble of wordplay as the curious, simple sound of a music box played six or seven measures and then stopped. It had to have come from the lumberjack's room.

I called him the lumberjack when, in truth, he simply trimmed trees and underbrush for the Native American settlement nearby. I didn't know his name. He made no attempts to be social, but I could certainly forgive such a failing. I had only seen him twice as I passed his open door. Once, he pushed the borrowed hotel vacuum and had his back to me. Medium build, sandy-haired. The second time, he stood in the middle of his studio apartment staring at something in his hand. I glanced in and out and kept walking. When you overhear every detail of your neighbor's routine from when he showers to his favorite television fare, you try not to make eye contact. It was a pretense of privacy. I'm certain he had not been holding a music box.

There I sat in the cold and dreary light of mid-March, caged in the menagerie that was the Hotel Toledo, and wondered what should be so unsettling about the sound of a music box. Sidney raised his head—possibly alert to the music, possibly attuned to the subtle tension in my arm. I soothed his head and neck, and reassured him that it was, again, none of our business.

"Let's take a walk," I said, and he jumped to the floor and cantered to the chair near the door. He sniffed at his leash and looked impatiently from me to it. "You're a good boy. So smart, aren't you?" Sidney bit playfully at the black nylon strap now hooked to his harness. He stuffed his nose in the crack of the door and waited eagerly for me to push it open.

In the hall, he tugged toward Dottie's open door while she chatted with a granddaughter about her plans for Easter. I stole a lingering look into her room. With Dottie's poor eyesight, she would never know. Her anonymity was preserved.

Through a series of stolen glances, I came to know Dottie's room intimately. Across the tiny space opposite the door sat a beige-pink sofa frozen in the fifties and preserved with doilies and preciously-gifted hand-made throws. The center cushion allowed just enough room for her to sit amidst a lifetime of memories—magazines stacked to her right, toiletries and a hand mirror trayed on the left. Behind the magazines, she'd propped an ornate plastic mirror. Next to it sat an emerald green glass bowl accumulating light bulbs, new or used. The deep windowsill showcased an array of pungent, half-empty perfumes, cheap but popular in whatever decade they were purchased. A small table sat in front of the sofa. In my neurotic desire to stay detached, I never let my eyes fall on that one tiny patch of living space. I can describe detailed patterns in the overlapping area rugs, the looped texture of the Herculon sofa, even the brick-orange shade of an opened tube of lipstick on the floor. But I never once let my eyes fall on the table top.

Dottie stood beside the table and talked more coherently than any ninety-five-year-old had a right to. Her thick, black shoes held tight against her support stockings. Her black dress—new in the fifties—hung just below her calves. In place of a jacket, she wore a vibrant purple blouse opened in the front and worn through at the elbows. Her painted nails matched the tinge of color at her lips which, in turn, echoed the smeared circles of rouge on each translucent cheek. She wore no eye makeup. Time, and failing health, had etched her lids and under-eyes the color of rust. White lashes fringed her ice blue irises—a strange counterpoint to an abundance of teased, auburn hair held away from her face by rhine-stone-covered plastic combs.

I tugged at the leash to pull Sidney away from the open door. He obeyed quickly, anxious to do his business in the bushes along the alley-way.

"Good morning, Carl," I said as we headed through the lobby.

Carl looked up from the mop he used to scrub the smell of smoke from the fractured marble floors. The strong odor of bleach mixed with the smell of tobacco and Dottie's talcum.

"Good morning, Mrs. Warner." Carl wheezed through his emphysema as his newest cigarette jumped up and down in his lips. He nodded at Sidney and smiled a little. "Kujo," he said, chuckling at a faded conver-sation. With some pride and trepidation, he added, "He may be small, but I bet he could lick any dog in this neighborhood."

"Maybe so," I agreed, "but then he trembles at the sight of a black trash bag on the curb." We both laughed, and I moved on past him toward the door.

Carl was afraid of dogs and only tolerated Sidney for the sake of his best tenant. I understood his feeling of unease, for I had the same trepidation about Carl. Accommodating as he was, Carl's temper could flare at the smallest provocation. The first time Sidney growled at him, we almost landed on the street. I patched the misunderstanding by secreting dog treats into Carl's hand at least once a week. The two of them held an uneasy truce. I trusted Sidney's judgment of the man and was wary myself when alone in the lobby.

I pushed through the front door and breathed in the small-town air, clearing the smell of smoke and solvent from my lungs. Sidney raised his own nose, sniffing out the latest information carried on the early spring breeze.

At times, we wandered the neighborhood in search of squirrels. He would scent their trails, or I would spot them in trees and point. Once cornered, the squirrels would flip their tails at the dancing dog straining at his harness. Occasionally, they would creep down the trunk, edge close enough to scold us for being so forward. We would walk the alleys and court house lawn, careful not to defile private yards. In the year we had been living in the hotel, Sidney and I had carved out our own private world in public view.

We turned right and headed south, down the street.

* * *

I dozed on the couch in front of the television. The usual two a.m. banter between infomercial hosts went silent, replaced by a low-pitched hum punctuated by an occasional tone that sounded hauntingly familiar. I pried my eyes open just enough to let in the light from the television screen. Pong. I closed my eyes and thought about sleep. Confused, I opened my eyes again, this time concentrating on the picture tube. The screen was black except for a vertical line along each side and one short line drifting back and forth between them. The wandering pixels of light hit the left side and sounded—*pong*—and then drifted to the right.

"What is that doing on my TV?" I asked in the wee hours. I lifted my head off the pillow and watched the small line bounce back to the left. Cell phone signals. Crossed wiring. I didn't understand it. I didn't care. I simply wanted to go back to sleep.

I pulled the pillow up under my head and tried to empty my thoughts again. Voices echoed from the lobby. Two, maybe three second-floor tenants were stumbling home from an alcoholic binge. They lingered a bit too long, and Carl soon called from his living quarters as he shooed the loiterers up the staircase. The laughter and footsteps faded slightly. Sidney stood up and shook himself, ringing his dog tags against each other, then circled a half dozen times and settled into his new sleeping position.

Marty must have been among the party animals, because his heavy steps entered the apartment above, and the door slammed shut. For the next thirty minutes, I watched a sideways game of Pong and listened to my upstairs neighbor heaving into the toilet. I remember hearing the two-thirty chime from the courthouse clock.

* * *

Someone once sent me a quote from one of those endless streams of Internet quotes circling the cosmos. "A person who learns from their mistakes is smart. A person who learns from other people's mistakes is smarter." Perhaps there was something I should be learning from these people.

"Carl!" Dottie's voice cried from the hallway in front of my door. Within seconds, Carl plodded toward our end of the hall.

"Isn't it a little hot in here?" Dottie whined artfully, hoping he would do her bidding.

"Now, Dottie, you know I have to keep it turned up for the tenants in the front of the building. I don't know why you can't open a window." Carl's firm-but-pleasant voice gave away his frustration.

"I don't want flies in my apartment."

"Dottie, it's too cold for the flies to be out."

"Then it's too cold for my window to be open!"

Bells rang out on Family Feud as Dottie and Carl came to the same impasse they reached four or five times as week. I grabbed for a newspaper to stir what little fresh air crept in my own open window. Two floors up, someone's woofers vibrated a trouncing beat down the iron girders that supported the building. Mumbling, Carl headed for the lobby again as the faint sound of a music box played beneath the radiator's mocking hiss. The tune was beautiful. And disturbing. It was so out of place.

The first time I hid from Dottie was by accident. I'd just gotten out of the shower and thought I'd heard tapping at my door. But in the hotel, it was hard to tell whose door and who was doing the tapping. I ignored it. Now there was no question. Dottie needed a collaborator in her struggle to control Carl. I patted the dog to keep him quiet and stayed planted on the couch. I could always say I'd been napping.

Dottie never knocked a second time. In that she was respectful.

"Carl!"

From the lobby I heard, "What do you want, Dottie?" Carl no longer hid his aggravation.

I searched for the tiny melody that had captured my attention earlier. Donnie Osmond chatted with the latest Pyramid celebrities as I turned to stone. Dottie must have won out, for an hour later, the room turned chill. Sidney stirred, wanting or needing to be walked. He pranced at the end of his leash as I opened my door. I turned toward the lobby and tugged Sidney forward. Just as we reached the lumberjack's door, Sidney stopped. He stood, hackles up, facing into the room. I could feel, more than hear, his low growl vibrating up the leash. As I caught up to him, Sidney began to bare his teeth.

Inside the room, Lumberjack faced the door while he inspected something shiny in his hand. I reined in the leash to get better control of Sidney and offered an apology.

"Sidney! Bad dog!"

Lumberjack smiled and said, "No problem." He reached for the door to push it closed just as Sidney lunged forward, stripping the leash through my fingers. I winced as it snapped taught against my wrist. In a rage, the dog snarled and barked furiously at the man's feet. Two more inches and he would have sunk his teeth into Lumberjack's shins. Stepping backward, I dragged Sidney out of the room. As soon as he was clear, the door slammed shut.

I hurried through the lobby, thankful that Carl wasn't sitting at the communal table. Perhaps he was puttering in the basement workshop or, hopefully, he had made his latest run to the Salvation Army Thrift Store to upgrade someone's furniture.

Once outside, I let Sidney sniff at the nearest patch of dried grass while I collected myself. Lumberjack had not flinched at Sidney's affront, but he could still turn us in. Carl needed very little excuse to evict a threatening dog. Though I could stand leaving this emotional abyss, I had no where else to go. I watched Sidney do his business and automatically pulled a plastic bag from my pocket. "No one else would let you in," I cautioned. "We have to be careful." I would promise to carry my companion in and out of the building. I would watch more carefully for opened doors. I would grovel at Carl's feet and plead Sidney's case.

I deposited the bag in the trash bin and cut the walk short as we retreated to the safety of our apartment.

* * *

A week passed, and Carl had said nothing. Lumberjack's door remained closed. Other than the dull ache in the pit of my stomach, life was back to normal.

I opened the door for our morning walk and found Carl standing in the hallway. He had a hand on Dottie's doorknob. I had second thoughts about who had been testing my own door and averted my eyes when Carl looked our way.

"Mornin' Kujo," he said as I worried about Sidney's demeanor. The dog simply walked up to Carl and wagged his tail. "I don't have anything for you, Sidney." Carl reached his hands out to show they were empty.

I relaxed my grip on the leash and forced a smile.

Carl pulled a newspaper from his jacket pocket and tried wedging it with the three others that were already pinched in the crack of Dottie's door. "She loves her sports," he said, chuckling under his breath. After a third try, he turned to me. "Have you seen Dottie lately?"

"No," I answered. "Maybe she's at her granddaughter's."

We waited until he had fitted the paper into the crack, and then Sidney and I squeezed past Carl and down the hall. It was one thing to meet him in the lobby, but the stories of his past stint in a Texas prison made close contact in small spaces quite unnerving. It was unfair to judge him,

I knew. As far as I could determine, he'd lived an exemplary life since buying the hotel.

The building was warped and shoddy, though Carl kept it bug free. Several of the walls were resurfaced in cheap material butted against the impressive woodwork and stone masonry of the original craftsmen. Bare fluorescent bulbs washed a sickly green glow across the cement gray paint that concealed intricate oak wainscoting. Once-elegant sleeping rooms had been dissected and recombined into small, awkward apartments paid for by the week. Eighty dollars bought little accommodation. I had taken more than one cold shower. I cooked meals on the only working burner on the stovetop. I could asked Carl to replace or repair it, but I was not inclined to invite him in.

Sidney insisted on turning north this particular morning. We walked up the hill and across the street to the courthouse lawn. We paraded around the lush green grasses that surrounded the county offices. An occasional face peered through the office windows and passed judgment on the comings and goings of us "hotel" people. A lawyer stepped from his office door and walked across the street toward the courthouse entrance. He smiled at us. I averted my eyes.

Sidney finished his business and reluctantly let me guide him back toward the hotel. We stepped into the lobby where a new tenant sat at the communal table and talked to Carl in a low voice. As soon as he saw us, he fell silent. Sidney strained to get closer to the man dressed all in black, wanting to sniff out information from his pant legs.

"Kujo," Carl mumbled past his smoking hand.

"Good morning," I said to the man in black and kept Sidney at a safe distance. So far the dog had not been inclined to judge the stranger at the table. When the new tenant failed to smile or reach toward Sidney in greeting, I pulled at the leash and started toward the hall.

Carl called after me. "Have you seen Gordon around lately?"

I stopped and turned back toward the lobby. "Gordon?"

"Your neighbor."

Ah, the lumberjack. "No," I said, afraid for what might be revealed about our last encounter. I stood like a schoolgirl waiting to be dismissed.

"He's three days overdue on his rent," Carl explained both to me and to the man in black. "That's not unusual for some, but it's not like Gordon. He's always been good bout takin' care a business, if you know what I mean." His manner of speech deteriorated into its colloquial pattern, indicating that he was no longer speaking to me. He reserved his most polite, if not condescending manner, for both Dottie and me—the two older women in residence.

Sidney wagged his tail and smiled a dog's smile as he turned down the hallway toward our sanctuary. When I stopped at my doorway, I noticed a faint smell—something sweet and sour and not quite pleasant. Dottie's door was ajar, but her lights were out. Even in the dim light I noticed that her sofa had been moved. I unlocked my own door and let Sidney run free into the apartment. Once inside, the smell grew stronger. I walked toward the kitchenette and glanced at the overflowing trash can. It was then I realized that, if not for Sidney and the consumption of food, I had no reason to leave the room I was standing in. I had come to this place to live out my anonymous life in semi-poverty. I could do nothing, be nothing for the rest of my life and never disturb anyone. If the walls didn't fall down around my head, I might still reside here in forty years, wearing the same navy blouse—worn through at the elbows—over the same black pants, my hair coiffed and orange, and demanding that Carl adjust the steam heat on my command. With great effort, I forced myself to bag the trash and carry it through the lobby and around back to the bin in the alley. I lifted the plastic corrugated cover on its hinge and tossed my refuse into the mix. It rolled past a cardboard box covered in reddish brown paint. Someone must have repainted their walls. I was sure Carl wasn't paying for it. When I returned to the kitchen, the smell was still there.

"I should wash the bottom of the can," I murmured to the dog. "Maybe later." I moved to the sofa and clicked on Jeopardy. Dottie's phone rang. No one answered it.

* * *

May began colder than usual. I shut my windows against the chill, holding in the stale air and magnifying the sweet malodor that pervaded my kitchen. I'd had enough. I pulled the plastic liner from the trashcan and tied it off. The can looked clean enough, but something had to be causing the stench. I walked through the bedroom and into the tiny bathroom shower. No use wasting precious hot water. Cold rain spattered against the side of the can and on to my face and arms. Just as I was about to turn out the excess water, someone pounded at a nearby door. Startled, I dropped the can on the shower floor.

"Gordon! You in there?"

I let my heart settle into a calmer rhythm and waited.

Carl beat harder at the hollow door, shaking the light bulb over my bathroom mirror. "Gordon!" he repeated, obviously angry. "I hear you in there!"

The wad of keys that hung from the retractable ring at Carl's waist rattled, and soon the lumberjack's door swung open. I finished my business and replaced the can in the kitchen. Sidney began to pace the floor, so I snapped on his harness, and we stepped into the hall. Carl was just exiting Lumberjack's apartment.

"God damn it," I heard him mumbling. When he saw me, he apologized. "Well, if Gordon skipped, he didn't take anything with him."

I shrugged my response and squeezed past him toward the lobby where Sidney and I vanished out the door.

* * *

Spring skipped to summer in less than a week, and soon everyone's windows were thrown open to the hot and humid wind. The sounds that previously had been muted by plaster and glass were magnified off the brick canyon walls of the downtown business district. Marty and Kristine were forced into a temporary truce but, occasionally, I would hear Marty's demeaning insults and Kristine's pouting apologies. They seemed more cautious knowing their biographies were open to the outside world.

"People have walked away, Kristine," I suggested to the ceiling.

Other tenants unknowingly shared their life stories with those us of who quietly listened. I made a distinction between conversations heard through walls and those cast callously out the open windows. The latter seemed fair game.

Sidney begged outdoors more frequently and, in the heat of the apartment, I was inclined to oblige. We would spend a few minutes chatting nonsense with whoever was about on the cool marble floors in the lobby. Most often it was Carl.

The newest tenant—the man in black—became a fixture at the communal table. As I walked Sidney through the lobby, I could detect a muted Eastern European accent that hushed as I entered the room. Carl would look up from the conversation and smile at me as I kept moving past them toward the outer doors. I was curious about the man in dark, tailored shirts, but not enough to intrude. As the outer doors closed behind me, I would catch a word or two in thick, broken English. A mystery. The hotel was full of mysteries. Including mine.

"Hey. You hear about the stabbing?" Carl asked in mid May.

I paused, wondering what seedy bar or crumbling neighborhood he might be talking about. Small town, small world. "No," I responded casually.

Carl shook his head. "You know your upstairs neighbors?"

"Oh, no!" I couldn't help but show my surprise and concern. "Is Kristine all right?"

Carl laughed causing his emphysema to kick up. When he had finished hacking and caught his breath, he explained, "Kristine said she was cooking and Marty was trying to grab the knife like he was playin'. Why, I don't believe that." He watched for my reaction. "She pushed the blade clean down to the bone."

I grimaced.

"You don't do that playin'. There's no way." Carl didn't wait for my response. "I told them to move on out. I don't want nothin' like that happenin' here, accident or no. I mean, I could use the rent, no doubt about it, but that's not so important as havin'," he gasp for air, "a safe place for the likes of you and Dottie to live. Don't you think?"

I was less surprised by the stabbing than Carl imagined I should be. Certainly, I thought a lot about where I lived and why. But I was no better than those I sat in judgment of. What made me different from my neighbors was how they lived their spare lives in the open while I cowered on the sidelines and pretended to be superior. Even Carl provided some service, meager as it was.

I caught my reflection in the Fifties speckled mirror tiles that covered ancient layers of lobby wallpaper. An oval face, with its narrow chin, was accentuated by extra weight around the jowls. Thin lips, unpainted. A narrow nose, with a decidedly off-center bump halfway to the bridge, rested between almond eyes once complimented by friends and lovers. Hair—boy short, neat, nondescript—carried more salt than pepper. Mine was the costume of obscurity.

"I'm sure Dottie will feel safer," I replied aloud to the ghost in the mirror, "but don't evict them on my account." I smiled at Carl and waded through self-pity toward the hall. "It's time to walk the dog."

I escaped to my rooms and stood frozen just inside the door as my despair drained the remaining color from my cheeks. I wanted to cry, but too much time had passed. Even Dottie, at ninety-five, had more life in her than I could possibly muster at that moment.

And then there was Kristine. The mouse had finally roared. "Good for you," I whispered. "You have a real chance now."

I heard an accusing voice bounce angry words off the alley walls followed by several whimpering apologies. "…medical bills we can't pay and now we're homeless!"

"I'm sorry, Marty. I'm sorry."

I shook my head and collapsed near Sidney. "I'm sorry, too, Kristine." Accident or intended, the mouse was still a mouse. And I was still a ghost. Dottie? The woman who demanded consideration and was not afraid to claim her space in the universe had been silent for much too long, it seemed. I began to worry about my neighbor.

* * *

It was my birthday. I walked Sidney and gave him an extra treat before locking him in the apartment. With my canvas bag, I walked three blocks to the corner store and picked out a week's worth of rations. Kristine stood at the checkout, paying for Marty's cigarettes. She didn't smoke. I walked up behind her and waited for the clerk to tally her goods and make change. I wanted to tell her how sorry I was, to give her a gem of wisdom that might nudge her toward some self respect. I said nothing.

The air had turned chilly again as it could in late May. I took my time walking back to the hotel. Delayed my penance.

"Mrs. Warner." Carl beckoned me into his office when I entered the lobby. "Have you seen hide ner hair of Dottie in a couple a weeks?"

"No," I told him.

"Somebody slipped her rent under my door, but I ain't seen nothing of her." Carl turned toward his personal quarters as if I'd never been in the room.

I stepped into the lobby and bumped directly up against the man in black. We both stepped back, and I apologized. He said nothing, but simply looked at my feet and waited for me to move out of the way.

I hurried down the hall, all the while throwing puzzle pieces together in my mind. The odd smell that had finally evaporated from my kitchen. The cardboard covered in brown paint in the trash. Dottie's disappearance. I shook off the notion of a dead body in the next apartment. Surely, she was fine. Somewhere. It was none of my affair to keep tabs on an old woman.

Later in the day, I heard Carl moving Lumberjack's things from his vacant apartment. He boxed and hauled the meager possessions to the old nightclub in the basement. I only hoped my new neighbor would be as easy to ignore. Carl would wait a few months and then sell Lumberjack's possessions to cover his lost rent. I would try not to wonder if Dottie was alive or dead and whether the man in black had had anything to do with her disappearance. I only had one charge. Sidney. And he gave infinitely more than he asked for.

* * *

His name was Bennie. Short for some Romanian name Americans would never pronounce correctly. He dealt black jack at the local casino. Fitting for the man in black. I pried what information I wanted from Carl. It mattered very little. Bennie had never warmed up to my vacant smile as I walked Sidney past him daily. Carl liked him, but I had to remember my own misgivings about Carl.

Dottie's sports pages hung and disappeared from her doorway again, but I'd not seen nor heard anything of her yet. It seemed odd that in the heat of summer she wasn't leaving her door open to allow for a breeze or fanning herself on the lobby sofa.

I threw the massive window sashes high and put my crock pot away for the summer. Marty and Kristine had moved on. The new girls in the apartment above weighed half as much as their footsteps implied. Young and impulsive, they threw parties on the weekends and played music until three in the morning. With no schedule of my own, I adapted my routine to their sleep patterns. It was easier than complaining to Carl.

The music box played for several measures before I picked it out from the background noise. As the cylinder rotated twice around and plucked its metallic tune into the air, I knew it was no longer in Lumberjack's old apartment.

Sidney came alert and let me know his wish to go out. I obliged him, stopping in the hallway long enough to listen for the compelling tune. Nothing. Sidney insisted on dragging me to the lobby. As anxious as he was for relief, he made time to check the floor under the communal table for crumbs from Carl's breakfast.

"You just missed the food, Sid," Carl said as he came out of the office.

"You spoil him." I realized that Carl's character was no longer an issue for me or the dog.

"Gotta keep Kujo happy," he said, and he reached down to rub Sidney's ears.

We walked into the summer air—shedding the oppressive heat of the hotel—and wandered into the grassy patch between the hotel and the alley. While Sidney sniffed out urban rabbit trails, I looked up at four floors of crumbling brick and mused over the thousand-plus stories the hotel had been privy to. In a time when the marble floors reflected their original opulence and newly fringed velvet dripped from the massive windows, the hotel would have been the social center of the universe in this tiny community. The flock-papered walls held their secrets, for sure, but the intimate lives of the wealthy patrons here would have had some sway over the outside world. The frayed and mismatched curtains that now hung from plastic rods and barely touched the peeling window sills served to hide today's tenants from the rest of humanity. Even in the open air, I could feel the barrier that isolated me from everyone and everything. I hauled poor Sidney inside sooner than he cared to go.

At the end of the hall, Dottie's door was open a foot or so. Sidney sniffed through the crack. I saw Dottie's black-skirted knee protruding from the welted edge of her fifties sofa and noticed the furniture had been restored to its original position—the wooden feet slumping into the old depressions in the carpet. Change was a frightening thing, sometimes.

I wanted to knock and say hello. I wanted to tell her that I thought she had been murdered so we could laugh about it. Instead, I pulled Sidney back and unlocked my door. Inside, I flipped through the handful of television channels until I could decide which innocuous program would require the least amount of thought. Dottie's phone rang. I practiced ignoring her one last time.

* * *

I began the day like any other. Numb. But in late evening, as I tuned into the TV game shows and social pabulum, my stomach ached ever more than normal. I drilled Alex Trebec's image into my head to erase the look on Dottie's face as they placed a pair of menacing handcuffs on her frail and shriveled wrists. She was barely surprised. I was stunned. She cried like an incorrigible youngster caught playing a naughty prank on a rival neighborhood child. She expressed no remorse, only frustration at the sting of threatened punishment.

At ten a.m., a police officer questioned me as he wrote down my irrelevant facts.

"No I.D.?"

"I don't drive," I said. "I've never had reason to get one."

I overheard conversations in the hall, and this time I strained to listen. Official voices remarked on the crime as they logged each piece of evidence and speculated on how long Lumberjack's body rotted away on the other side of my kitchen wall while Dottie chopped off pieces small enough to wrap in the sports pages that Carl had so dutifully supplied. How could Carl not know? And here I stood—nearer to Dottie's life than anyone, and most ignorant of all.

At ten after ten, Carl appeared wanting solace. "I just can't believe it," he kept repeating as he wandered, uninvited, to my sofa and sat down. Sidney jumped up beside him. Carl paid him no mind as the dog's muzzle rested on his paws and his eyes flirted from me to Carl and back. I could have used Sidney as an excuse to escape outside, but I stood near the bedroom door and watched Carl wrestle with Dottie's stunning deed. "I just don't believe it. Do you? Why would she even do something like that?"

I shrugged and said nothing.

"*How* could she? Why, I know she's healthy as a horse," Carl continued as he talked his way in circles and tried to explain away his incredulity.

She was old. Too old. She was stubborn beyond belief. Yes, she was strong, but Gordon had to be stronger. He was such a nice guy.

"Can you even believe it?" Carl asked for the tenth time. "Why, even if she was strong enough, ya know," his head shook sideways as he talked, "why on earth would she ever do such a damn thing as this, pardon my language? I've known Dottie for years. She's never even so much as looked crossed-eyed at anyone."

"Dementia?" I asked aloud, grasping at anything to placate Carl.

The strain on his face eased just a bit. It was an excuse he could live with. "Yeah," he said. "Maybe so." For Carl, Dottie was more than a tenant. She was part of a mystique that Carl clung to regarding his precious hotel. He would never have tolerated their quarrels, the games she played, had it not been for Dottie's grande dame status. She represented the glory days of the Hotel Toledo. Without Dottie, the hotel was little more than a collection of rogues, drunkards and shameless personalities.

I tapped at Sidney's leash. On cue, he jumped off the couch and started whining. We escorted Carl to the lobby and escaped out the front door. To Sidney's delight, I kept him outside until I was sure Carl had retreated into his office. Then, carefully, we threaded our way back through the activity that ran the length of the hall and returned to our rooms.

An hour later, a persistent knock forced me to open my door to the glare of a flood light as a faceless cameraman and a clown-faced reporter crammed into the tiny space between Dottie's door and mine.

"How well did you know the accused?" The microphone swung toward me and threatened to dislodge my teeth. "Do you have any idea why Mrs. Rayburn might have wanted to harm Mr. Munson?"

Rayburn. Munson.

"How long have you lived here, uh," she checked her notes, "Mrs. Warner, is it?"

I flushed at such a public mention of my alias.

Inside Dottie's apartment, near the kitchenette, a gloved officer placed something heavy into a plastic evidence bag. Dottie's skillet—the cast iron she lifted every day like a training weight when she cooked her meals. In shameful silence, her grandson Billy sat on the doilied sofa, his head in his hands, obviously trying to get his thoughts around his grandmother's guilt. A uniformed officer scurried past him, tidied up what the police had deemed unimportant.

No longer hiding my curious gaze, I ran my eyes around the familiar room. The cloyingly-sweet perfumes were gone from the windowsill. For the first time I realized the window to the left, tucked behind one end of the sofa, was not a window but a door . The position of the sofa blocked the knob and deadbolt. Through the dust-colored glass, I could just see the top of the dumpster in the back alley.

I began to wonder what else I had missed, and then I saw it. In plain sight of Billy's grief, in the middle of the tiny table that held up Dottie's daily living, sat a silver music box. No one paid it any mind.

Was that it, I asked myself. *Was there no better reason to carve the life from someone?*

"I have something on the stove," I said and closed the door on the one-eyed cameraman and his mouthpiece.

From the hall, I heard the reporter's voice stab through my paper-thin ego. "Cooking what, I wonder." Her callous and accusing whispers resonated through the door. "She heard and saw nothing? Right. I wonder what her story is."

My story. I was not yet ready to tell it. Perhaps at the age of ninety-five I would no longer care if I was carted off in handcuffs, but on this day, there had been too many revelations. Dottie would certainly lose her freedom. Trapped by my cowardice in a prison of my own making, I had to ask, "Would I know the difference?"

Chapter Two

Hotel Toledo was a hellish place in summer. There were days when I suffered the heat in a tee shirt and shorts only to peel those meager threads off in the dark of night and stretch across the top sheet covering the bed. I stationed a box fan facing outward in the window to push the stale air into the alley while a second fan spilled muggy heat directly across my legs and bare back. Even Sidney could no longer stand to lie beside me. He shifted fitfully from position to position, panting desperately. When I finally dragged myself from bed in late morning, I welcomed the cold showers which were a staple of hotel living.

Fourth of July had come and gone. The police had cleared Dottie's room of evidence and Billy was packing the last of his grandmother's belongings to be stored at his home until the family could distribute keepsakes and mementos. The furniture would stay.

That part of my past that held me here kept threatening to expose itself. There were days when I knew everyone suspected me of something. Admittedly, the hotel tenants now suspected every other tenant on principle. That was Dottie's legacy.

Sidney asked to go out. I pulled on my dirty white sneakers and slipped a bra beneath my shirt. The lobby sat empty as we headed toward the outer doors. Sidney pulled in the direction of the courthouse, but I held him back. Lawyers and clerks doing business in the county offices no longer welcomed us with smiles. Guilt by association. I pulled Sidney toward the back alley.

When we returned to the lobby, Carl sat at the table while he ate his microwaved lunch and read a newspaper. "Hey, Mrs. Warner. Did you read the want ads in the shopper today?"

"No," I admitted and decided to have a seat across from him.

"It's the damdest thing, pardon me," he said with a chuckle and began to read. "'Mystery writer looking for research material.'" Carl breathed a little heavy as he spoke. "'My character needs to get away with a murder. Strictly confidential.'" He rolled his eyes. "Prob'ly cops lookin' to catch some idiots like they do on them giveaway stings they pull ever so often."

I maintained a blank expression.

"I'd send this to Dottie," Carl said, only half joking, "but she really didn't get away with it, now did she?" He screwed his face up and shook his head. "Damn, I still can't believe it."

I glanced at Sidney who lay on his side to take full advantage of the cool marble. He seemed willing to spend more time, so I asked if I could take a look at the shopper. I turned to the front page and took my time wandering through the ads and classifieds. When I stumbled on the mystery writer's request, I read and reread the address. Casually, I slid the paper back to Carl's side of the table and stood to leave.

"I was wondering," I ventured to ask, "do you have anyone interested in Dottie's apartment yet?"

"Well, no actually." Carl's lungs whistled as he drug the air in and out with great effort. "Nobody wants to go the extra ten bucks a week for the separate kitchen. Least, that's what they say. Why? You interested?"

"I think I would be," I said. "I could take Sidney directly out into the alley without worrying who was in the lobby."

Carl raised an eyebrow. "You havin' a problem with anyone in particular?"

"No," I assured him. "But if you ever had another tenant with a dog, they wouldn't have to cross paths."

"Why, sure," Carl agreed. "You still have to bring him 'round for his treats, though."

"Certainly," I said. I tugged the reluctant dog up from the marble. "Let me know when it's ready."

"Be ready tonight, if you want."

"Maybe tomorrow." I thanked him and walked back to my room. Once inside, I found a scrap of paper and jotted down the address I had been repeating in my head. I stared at the paper and wondered what to do with it. With no clear idea, I pulled open my purse and tucked it away where it would sit a few days and then be pitched with the garbage. Surely.

Since Dottie's arrest, the nights in the hotel had taken on a different tone. Noises once ignored seemed to scream through the quiet hours. Most tenants were asleep after two a.m., but often I could hear the padding of footsteps toward someone's bathroom or the sound of restless feet as someone tried to out-pace the heat. More often, the noises came from the building itself as it settled a micron at a time into the dirt. When the girls upstairs would tread carelessly, bits of plaster would flake and rain down on top of the suspended ceiling tiles over my head. I stifled the urge to cover my hair.

I gave up sleeping when the sky showed signs of daylight. It was only five a.m., but I had things to do this particular day. Sidney watched me from the bed as I pulled my clothes from the borrowed dresser drawers and stuffed them into a large trash bag. I found a small plastic tub in one corner of the closet and gathered my toiletries into it. It seemed strange to pack for such a short move. As quickly as I could box the handful of items I used each day—shampoo, soap, a comb, toilet paper—I could walk them into the new bathroom. In the kitchen, I added a handful of eating utensils and the few pantry items.

Five-thirty. Too early to wake Carl. I sat on the sofa and clicked on the television. "…four easy payments…you'll never have to scrub again…cut your cooking time in half…" I clicked the television off again.

A weight heavier than I could bear descended around me. I was half Dottie's age, and yet I felt so very old. I looked around the shoddy rented room at the worn rented furniture next to the rusting rented appliances. In the middle of the sloping floor, a small plastic tub and a black trash bag held everything I could claim as my own. No *Billy* waited to parcel out my mementos. I had no mementos. Even Lumberjack had owned a music box. It suddenly mattered to me who would get the shiny stolen treasure. I had said nothing, and now the ornate silver box was destined to pass down through the wrong family.

My thoughts shifted from the music box to a hand-blown glass bowl, beautifully elegant and rich with color. The bowl represented my own bloody secret, and it made me laugh. I laughed so hard my eyes began to water. Sidney came in from the bedroom and sat beside me on the couch while my laughter turned to sobs and then again to howls of amusement. My shoulders shook hard with the release of emotion. Soon I was spent and laying sideways on the cushions. Sidney licked my fingers, tasting the salt tears I'd wiped from my face.

I fell asleep by the time Carl knocked at my door.

"Mrs. Warner? You need any help movin'?"

I cracked the door a few inches and assured him that I didn't.

"Here's the new keys. Just get me the old ones when yer done."

I thanked him and closed the door again. I wiped down the sinks and counters—not that anyone could tell much difference—and made a last check of the rooms before stepping across the hall. Sidney wandered straight into Dottie's living room, glad to finally satisfy his curiosity about the place.

"This is your new home, Sidney." I glanced at the beige pink sofa and made a mental note never to buy a doily. The dog started to lift his leg in an effort to claim his new territory, but I scolded him just in time. "We don't pee where we sleep. Remember that."

The living area was larger than my previous one. The windows to the alley sat lower in the wall and provided a better view of the world.

"Don't buy doilies, and don't walk around naked."

Sidney stopped to glance at me and then headed off again.

Across the room, an opening with abandoned hinges and striker plate led into a tiny kitchen. The cabinets were layered in dirty gold paint that showed hints of two previous colors. I could sand and paint them easily enough if I wanted to spend the money. The counter tops and stove were in reasonably good shape. I could see now that I would reap the benefits of Dottie's demanding personality.

Right of the kitchen was a closed door leading to what had to be the bedroom and bath. I turned the knob and pushed the door open. Sidney ran ahead, thrilled at the thought of having adventures without his leash. He stopped inside the door and sniffed at the carpet. When he didn't move out of the way, I reached around to flip on the overhead fixture. The dark, paneled walls sucked up most of the light, and I waited for my eyes to register the new surroundings. Sidney began to dig at the carpet with his teeth. I shooed him the rest of the way into the room.

"Stop that!" I chastised him. "I'll feed you soon enough. You don't have to eat…" I froze in awe and disgust. Sidney turned back to the carpet and continued to sniff at the perimeter of a large stain. The color of rust paint on cardboard. I saw Lumberjack's broken head spilling out his life while Dottie teetered on her heavy black shoes as she gripped a skillet in one hand and touched the wall for support with the other. Any hint of morbid curiosity I might have had was soon swept away by waves of nausea. I ran to the bathroom and fumbled for a light switch. Thanks to Dottie's stubborn will, the fixtures in the bathroom looked new. This distracted me enough to get control over my rebellious stomach. I leaned into the sink and waited until the nausea had passed. When Sidney pawed at the stained carpet again, I ordered him to stop.

The face in the mirror sported a number of scars. Some were physical, healed over and no longer painful. Others were emotional, half buried but still raw to the touch. My eyes were dull—tired and puffy from my early morning sob fest. I contemplated asking for my old rooms back. Once again, I found myself the victim of bad choices and resigned that I would stay. This was where I belonged—halfway between the living and the dead.

Penance comes in all flavors. Mine was to live in a tired hotel in a room that carried the pall of death. For the first few days, I used the alley door exclusively to take Sidney outside. I couldn't face anyone, especially not Carl who would be watching me curiously. I lived out of the trash bag, refusing to put my clothes into the dresser in the bedroom. I laid a towel over the stain and only walked over it on my way to the restroom. I slept on the sofa, but that was not unusual. I watched television. Obsessively, I cleaned the kitchen.

By the end of that week, I was down to a can of tuna and a box of crackers. I showered and changed into my last set of clean clothes and quietly locked Sidney in the room. When I was reasonably certain no one was about, I walked through the hotel and into the glare of the summer sun. The quiet of the street marked a lull in the town's activity.

At the local market, I selected my usual rations. While digging for change, I found a stray piece of paper with an address on it. I stared at it a moment and then poked it back into a side pocket. I finished paying and stepped outside. When the light on the corner turned green, I turned right instead of left and walked to the courthouse lawn. Comfortable that no one was paying me any mind, I sat on a bench and slipped the paper from my purse again. I folded and unfolded the scrap several times. My inner voice argued that responding to the ad was as idiotic as Carl knew it to be. I should have tossed it in the trash, but something about Dottie's recent escapade lit a spark inside my coward's heart. Even Kristine's brief attempt to assert herself shamed me.

I stood up from the bench and walked back across the street and past the market. A block and a half more stood the newly-renovated town library. I slipped inside.

The exterior doors opened into a large, echoing lobby. At the far end, near a second set of doors to the library proper, was a large glass case. I stopped at the case to gather my courage and to practice my sideways glances. Just inside the main library entrance, on the right, was the check-out desk occupied by only one librarian. Directly in front of her were a handful of computer stations, some of them populated. I stared back at the display in front of me as I pretended to read placards about a *butter lady* famous for sculpting farm animals out of milk fat. The sculptures were quite good, actually. Just buttery.

After staring dumbly at the grainy photos for several minutes, I pulled open the second door. Eyes ahead, I marched past the librarian's desk and into the newly-constructed wooden stacks. The smell of construction glue and cut lumber permeated row after row of alternating classics or new releases. I turned left down the center aisle and found a row that kept me safely out of view of the woman fussing over the latest returns.

"Now what?" I ventured to ask the many plastic-covered book titles. I pulled a few books off the shelf and pretended to leaf through them or read the jacket reviews. I turned down another row and caught sight of the computer stations again. Too many people. I toyed with the idea of checking out a book before remembering my status as a nobody. I replaced the book in my hand and walked back toward the exit. Near the desk, the librarian looked up from her chores.

"Can I help you find anything?"

"No thank you," I said and kept moving—past the desk, through the double doors, past the butter cow lady and, at last, to freedom. My knees shook the entire walk back to the hotel. I chastised myself for playing into my fear and yet delighted in the energy it created. I felt more alive than I had in years. I knew then that I would have to write the letter. No matter what.

* * *

The last week of July set new heat records. Sidney and I walked in early morning and late evening, but during the horrid heat of midday, I left him in front of the fan and escaped to the library to spend time in the air conditioning.

My fourth day there, I found the computer stations unattended. I sat down at the one that gave me the clearest view of the room. It had been a while, but I found my way into a word processing program. Before I could type a word, a motherly voice said, "You need to sign in to use the computers."

Startled, I looked up at the librarian who, I was sure, had not been behind the desk just moments before.

"I was just looking for a website," I explained, surprised at how meek my voice sounded.

She smiled generously and said, "That's no problem. We just ask that anyone using the computers sign in and note the time. We keep track in case it gets busy so everyone can have a fair turn." She pointed toward a clipboard.

I stood and walked toward the counter. When I picked up the pen, I realized that I had no full name to give her. For almost two years, I had been Mrs. Warner. Carl did not require a written lease and had never asked my first name. Worried that I had hesitated too long, I looked further up the list and found a name that would suit my purposes. I quickly scribbled *Mary Warner* and logged in the time. The librarian motioned me back toward the computer.

"I'm Zoe, if I can be of any help." Her smile was genuine, but her eyes were clouded with sadness, perhaps weariness. For the first time, I noticed her hair. Thin and weak. Chemo, most likely. I wanted to ask and perhaps offer sympathy, but I didn't want to intrude. I never wanted to intrude, so I simply walked back to the computer and sat down.

After familiarizing myself with the different options, I settled on a font and began to type, "Dear Mystery Writer." I stared at the screen for another few minutes before continuing. "I'm writing in response to your want ad. I have knowledge of a crime that was committed some years ago." I read the last sentence through a few times and then backspaced and rewrote, "I have certain knowledge that I would be willing to share. What kind of information do you think would be most helpful?"

I could have told my story then and been done with it. I knew the risks, but something in me craved the interaction. I added, "I do so enjoy reading the shopper. Yours truly, Anonymous Research Assistant." I leaned back and stared at the words on screen. The act of writing the note, even unsent, changed me at that moment. This mystery writer, anonymous as a priest, would hear my confession and, perhaps then, I could take back my life. When Zoe was free, I walked up to the counter.

"How can I print off a letter I've written?"

Zoe started out from behind her desk.

I panicked. "No, I mean, I know how," I said quickly, "but where does it print out?"

"Oh." Zoe turned back to the desk. "Just hit print, and I'll hand it to you."

"Okay." I turned away before she could see my cheeks flush.

At the computer, I opened the letter again and wondered if I should hit the delete button. Surely, Zoe wouldn't dare read the page right in front of me. What did it say after all? Nothing incriminating. I held my breath and clicked *print*.

I emptied the word processor of what I'd written and closed it down. At the counter, I waited for the hum of the machine to stop. Zoe reached for the page and handed it over without a glance. Just as quickly, I folded it in half and tucked it into my purse. I thanked her, paid her a dime for the copy and walked as casually as I could from the library back to the hotel.

Sidney didn't get up but simply greeted me with a sideways thump of his tail. I stripped off my street clothes and pulled on a tee shirt and shorts. Before I could settle on the sofa and open my purse, someone knocked at the door.

"Mrs. Warner?" Carl called in his rasping voice.

"Just a minute," I answered and threw an oxford shirt over my tee. When I opened the door, Carl stood in the hall holding my Crock Pot.

"You left this in the other apartment. You still want it, right?"

"Oh, yes," I said, taking the slow cooker from his hands. "Thank you."

"Yeah, well, a new guy moved in last night and he found it in the cupboards. A Mr. Varble. Retired fella I think."

"I'm glad you could rent it out so quickly."

"Well, seems all the apartments go pretty quick." He drew in a long breath and grimaced at the effort. "'Cept this one. I appreciate you makin' the move. How's it working out?"

"It's good," I told him. To change the subject, I asked, "How often does the county shopper come out?"

Carl coughed twice and sucked in air. "Once a week. On Wednesdays. We got a new one up front if you want a look at it."

"No, thank you anyway. I was just getting ready for a nap. But don't throw them away when you're done with them." I started to close the door.

"You lookin' for work?"

The question caught me off guard. There were only three reasons to read the shopper—to buy something, to sell something, or to look for work. Four if you counted the personals. "I was thinking I might check around," I said casually. "Not that I need the money."

"The casino's always hirin'. Maybe you could check out there."

"I'll look into it. Thanks again." This time I managed to get the door closed before another word was spoken. I hurried to the sofa and retrieved the letter from my purse. *I have certain knowledge* it read in pica ten-point type.

Sidney rolled over to cool his other side in front of the fan while I stared, unblinking, out the windows and into the treetops until the images of separate trees fused into one jittery mass of green and blue. "Was I sure?" I asked myself, but I knew the answer. My only question now was where to mail the letter from. Not the hotel, certainly, and not from Toledo. Maybe the casino? I would need envelopes and stamps.

A few minutes later I heard an unsettling rattle at my door. I waited for someone to knock, but whoever was in the hall did not announce himself. When everything was silent again, I quietly opened my door. Something fell to the floor. At my feet lay the county shopper.

* * *

Sidney walked into an uncut patch of grass and began pulling up the blades with his teeth. After he'd plucked a mouthful, he patiently waited for the greens to settle his stomach.

"I understand, buddy," I told him, feeling queasy in the unrelenting August heat. When he moved again, I followed his lead.

It had been two weeks since I'd taken one of the infinite number of tour buses that ferried gamblers to and from Ames, Iowa. I began my journey by walking to a local motel and waiting for a free shuttle that catered to the casino patrons. My intent had been to post the letter from there, but it required handing the envelope over to a desk clerk, and still the letter would have been postmarked from Toledo. Instead, I waited at the curb and stepped onto the next charter bus heading west.

I don't remember the parking lot in Ames where the driver pulled to a stop. My mind was cued to the free-standing mailbox on the sidewalk a few yards away. I slipped off the bus with the departing passengers, walked casually to the box, and dropped the letter through the slot. Just as casually, I walked to the end of the line of new passengers waiting to board. In two days time some literary wanna-be would slice the envelope open and perhaps find something of interest. I would dutifully read through the papers that Carl now fitted regularly into the crack of my door.

Sidney walked to a patch of grass between the sidewalk and the street and lay down. I let him rest for a moment or two and then tugged him to his feet. "Time to go, buddy." We took our time climbing the slight slope of the hotel grounds toward the front door.

Inside, Carl read the bi-weekly town paper which snapped back and forth each time he rattled out a cough.

"Good morning, Carl."

"Hey, Mrs. Warner. Hey, Sidney." Carl reached down to scratch the dog behind the ears while I pulled out a chair and sat down. "You had any luck with a job?" he asked me.

"Not really. I'm not sure if I want to work. I don't really need the money."

Carl pulled his upper body back in his chair. Even this slight move created an obvious strain on his face. He laid his smoking hand on the table and watched a stream of nicotine rise in a column from the burning leaf. "I been meanin' to ask you, if it's not pryin', just where you get yer money. You retired already?" He leaned in again and took a short drag from his cigarette. "You ain't old enough to be collectin' Social Security, are ya?"

I said nothing about my inability to claim what was rightfully mine. Instead, I glanced down at Sidney asleep on the pitted marble tiles. We sat in silence for a while, staring at the dog or the paper or out the lobby doors.

Over the next few days, I left Sidney alone more than I should have. He suffered in the oppressive heat of the hotel while I retreated to the cool recesses of the library's reading nooks. As an apology, I managed to bring him a small treat each afternoon.

Zoe worked most days. When she was alone behind the desk, I would linger a bit and ask about a particular book I'd picked from the shelf. She seemed eager to chat and yet her manner was restrained.

One Wednesday afternoon, I walked in to see a bald-headed woman leaning over a stack of newly-returned books. I hoped the flush on my face would be taken as a reaction to the late August heat. Perhaps it was, or perhaps Zoe had grown accustomed to the awkward reactions from library patrons and people she passed on the streets. I could pretend all was normal, or I could mention the obvious. Something in me was tired of pretending.

"Zoe. All formality aside, and if it's not prying, may I asked how you are doing?" To my relief, she relaxed her posture and leaned a little more in my direction.

"Pretty good, really. My doctor says the tumors have stabilized. They're not shrinking, but they're not growing either." She described the latest round of treatments and what might be next. She finished the conversation as though we'd been talking about her health for months. Her words, her tone of voice filled the moment with hope, but the shadow never lifted from her eyes. Life for Zoe was in a terrible limbo. To some small degree, I knew how that felt.

I walked home to find the *County Shopper* skillfully wedged into the crack of my door. Inside, Sidney stood anxious and hungry. After a brief walk, I made him sit for his supper, and then I curled onto the sofa and began scouring the columns of ads in the personals section. Halfway down the page, I found what I was looking for.

"Anonymous Research Assistant: What evidence was destroyed and how? My character needs a clean get away! Confidentially, MW."

As I read the words, my mind raced ahead to the many possible conclusions to this daring distraction. So far, I had done nothing to jeopardize my anonymity. Why should I tamper with my current state of affairs?

I looked around the tiny, sterile room with its shoddy paneling and exposed piping. I laid the paper off to one side and began to compose my response. Details. He wanted details. It would require dredging up some very painful memories, but I was committed to excising my ghosts. My confessor would hear it all.

* * *

At three in the morning, the television scrambled to snow, and I started awake on the couch. I flipped channels to find that they were all dancing with static. The first breath of cool air I'd felt in weeks wandered in through the open window. Along with the breeze came the smell of garbage. Sidney looked up from the floor.

"I guess I've worn the poor thing out," I said, rubbing his ears briefly. I clicked the off button, and the room went dark.

Someone above dropped their feet to the floor and padded toward a restroom. Private noises filtered through the plaster and timber, and then the footsteps retreated again. Soon, there was a mind-numbing silence about the place.

By nine a.m., I had not moved, nor had I gone back to sleep. My eyes traced the edges of several stains in the ceiling tiles and counted the number of nails that had been used to secure the sagging squares. Shoddy workmanship. Carl's resources were limited by the caliber of tenant he could attract which, in turn, was restricted by the ambiance of the rooms, which, inevitably, came back to the quality of repairs done over the years. Still, for an ex con, he carried his own weight.

At one minute after nine, I sat up. Sidney raised an eyebrow in my direction to see if I would move toward the kitchen. When I didn't, he simply wet his nose and closed his eyes again.

I reached for my purse and pulled up the lining where I'd torn it loose many months before. Inside, I retrieved some of the money stashed there. Fanning the bills, I made a mental note of how I would use them in the next few days. Four crisp hundreds would cover a month's rent and buy food for both Sidney and I. The last bill, precious for the freedom it represented, would pay my way to another distant mail box. It was a lot to risk in both money and security.

After Sidney had been walked and fed, I headed straight to the library. Zoe was not about. I signed in using my alias and sat at my usual console. I opened two programs, minimizing one that I could retrieve if someone came too close. Alone in the corner, I set to work typing in the details I had tortured over in the early morning hours. The letter would have to be worded carefully to keep the authorities off my trail if this brazen author did turn out to be a hoax.

Dear Mystery Writer,

First, I must tell you that this was a crime of passion, and though the killer was never jailed, he or she has suffered greatly over the years for what they have done.

For the sake of storytelling, I will say that the killer was a man. The victim, a woman. No charges were ever filed because no body was found. The man claimed the woman had simply run off, and authorities could find no evidence of foul play in the home.

Let's just say the argument was over money. There had never been any violence between them, although, in the last few months they were together, they argued frequently.

The night in question was a holiday. The killer had just bought the woman a gift of little value—an afterthought rather than a display of affection. This began an argument that lasted several hours. While the accusations were flying, the woman accused the man of having no ambition. He slapped her. She hit back. In the ensuing struggle, he grabbed the nearest object and hit her on the head.

This is where the killer's luck becomes a major player. Lucky for him, anyway. The blunt object was a paperweight he had made in his studio. He was a glass blower.

Auspiciously, there was little blood from the wound. There was a small amount on the globe, but most of the hemorrhaging appeared to be internal. The killer quickly placed a trash bag between the woman's head and the carpet where she'd fallen. He took the globe to the garage and placed it in with his glass stock. He fired up the furnace and returned to the kitchen. Under the sink, he located a pair of rubber gloves and put them on.

His second stroke of luck was the unfinished barbeque pit in the yard. The couple had exchanged many cross words over the fact that the hole had been dug months before but was filling with leaves and debris. Sacks of concrete and mortar sat beside pallets of unused brick.

Returning to the living room, the killer wrapped the victim's head in the bag and carried her to the trench. He carefully scooped the dead leaves to one side and, after laying her in, covered her with dirt and more leaves.

His next order of business was to fabricate a reason for her disappearance. A computer-generated suicide note or letter of goodbye would hardly fool her relatives. He located the personal journal she kept in her dresser and thumbed through the pages. On several pages he found lengthy essays about her desire to leave him. He chose one that sounded particularly like a goodbye letter and cut it from the journal, folding it into a small envelope.

Next, the killer systematically collected clothing and several of the woman's favorite things. In the garage, he cut her suitcase into small pieces and patiently fed them into the now-hot furnace. He burned her clothes, under-wear, shoes—anything that she might have taken with her. Finally, he tossed the journal into the inferno.

He washed his hands in the utility sink, scrubbing with bleach and soap.

Returning to the furnace, he grabbed a gathering ball and collected a scoop of glass and the paperweight and fed them into the heat. The blood on the paperweight was quickly burned away. When all the pieces had merged into a pool of molten glass, he reached his blow pipe into the fires. Carefully he spun, puffed and turned the glass—stretching its shape. When he had finished the piece, he cut it from the pipe and placed it in the cooling kiln.

The only remaining evidence was a collection of jewelry that he eventually melted and used to decorate the edge of the exquisite glass bowl.

When all the other evidence was cleared away, he rolled a wheel barrow from the garage to the debris-filled grave site. With the garden hose close by, he mixed and poured barrow after barrow of concrete into the hole until he'd filled and troweled a base for the final layer of brick and mortar which he finished two days later.

The police investigated after the victim's mother had reported her missing. The killer showed them the note and let them search the house. They questioned him several times about her disappearance, but he was never charged.

Though the case was never solved, know that the killer lives in his own private hell.

Yours truly, Your Humble Research Assistant.

I sat back in the chair and reread the letter only once. I was afraid that, if I began editing, I would lose the impetus to send it. I hit the print button.

CHAPTER THREE

It was mid-September. The heat let up, promising a pleasant Fall, but I had difficulty sleeping. Without the television's masking noise, I heard every snap of timber, every footstep, every joyous or cross word spoken anywhere in the building. I listened intently to who came in and out of the lobby, waited for some cold, official voice to question Carl on the whereabouts of *the women in this picture*. Afraid of my own shadow, I closeted myself in my room and tried to think of some way out of my little melodrama. When I could stand it no more, I slipped out through my personal exit and headed for the library.

Zoe greeted me with a warm smile and a full head of short, thick hair.

"Wow!" I said, unable to stop myself. "You look great. How is the treatment going?"

"Good," she said with a dismissive smile. "I haven't seen you in a while."

"I've been busy." After a long pause, I asked, "Anything new I should be reading?"

"Yes, actually. I'd recommend *Peace Like a River*. I just finished it, and it's really good." She headed into the stacks as I followed, dutifully. When she pulled the book and placed it in my hands, she said, "Why don't you get a library card so you can take this with you?"

I turned the book over a couple of times. "I can't," I admitted. "I don't have I.D."

"Nothing with your picture on it?"

After years of isolation, I let Zoe into my space. "None that I can share with you."

She raised an eyebrow and then nodded to reassured me that she would pry no further.

"Besides," I said with a weak laugh, "it's cooler here."

Zoe walked me over to my usual reading chair and left me to digest my own thoughts. After fighting the first few lines of the book, I was soon swept up in a story of violence, family ties and the supernatural nature of God's love. What seemed like only moments later, Zoe tapped me on the shoulder and told me the library was closing. I slipped a small scrap of paper into my place, returned the book to the shelf and left for the hotel.

I braved the lobby to find Carl smoking and sipping a soda in his usual spot at the communal table. "Hey there, Mrs. W," he said, chuckling at his own cleverness. "I haven't seen you and Sid around much lately. Everything all right?"

I sat across from him and leaned onto the table top. "I've been a little under the weather. I'm feeling better now."

Carl looked concerned. "Well, now, you just let me know if there's ever anything you need from the store like medicine or somethin'." A vague look of melancholy flashed across his face. "I used to get stuff for Dottie all the time. She was a pistol." He shook his head. "Thing is, I miss the livin' daylights out of her."

I envied Carl. He had someone to care about and who, even from prison, must have cared about him. It struck me then, the happenstance that prison was something he and Dottie now had in common.

"Have you heard from Dottie? How is she doing?"

Carl looked eager to answer. "I went to see her the other day. Got permission and drove all the way to Oakdale." He saw my blank expression. "They got a medical unit there. Prob'ly put her there 'cause she's so old, and all." He smiled a little and said with some admiration, "She was lookin' pretty good for being in such a place. They must be treatin' her pretty well."

"I'm glad to hear that," I said for his sake. I shook off the recurring image of Lumberjack's broken head forever laying on what was now my bedroom floor. "Has Dottie ever said why she did it?"

"Nope," Carl stated sharply. "I even asked her that. She just looks kinda dazed and says 'What's past is past.' Even Billy can't get nothin' out of her. I'm just hopin' she lives comfortable in whatever time she's got left. Prison can be pretty hard on anybody." He lowered his eyes.

I looked at Carl's face and wondered how many years of hard labor were etched there. The gray in his hair extended into his two-day-old beard and even into the flesh that hung from his sunken cheekbones. I had blamed cigarettes for his poor health, but perhaps they were only part of the story. "Carl?"

"Yeah?" he said, looking up from his moment of introspection.

"Could you find me a really cheap television?" I watched his eyes light up a bit.

"Sure. I can probably pick somethin' up next time I'm at the Goodwill. They usually have a few. How much you want to spend?"

I shrugged. "Can I get something for less than thirty dollars? It doesn't have to be much."

Carl's shoulders straightened. "Thirty bucks, I can get you something pretty good. I'm going up Thursday. That soon enough?"

"Plenty," I said and gave him an appreciative smile.

I excused myself from the table and headed down the hall to take Sydney for his walk. As soon as I had him harnessed and stepped into the hall, the door to my old apartment flew open and an elderly man, eyes glaring, stood silent in the doorway.

"You must be Mr. Varble," I ventured.

Sidney pulled forward toward the familiar space. As soon as he reached the threshold, Mr. Varble kicked at Sidney, lifting the dog slightly off the ground and sending him backward. In a rage, Sidney scrambled to his feet and went after the aggressor. A second kick sent Sidney yelping against the door jam. By then, I had reeled in the leash to get Sidney out of harm's way. I picked him up and held him tightly in my arms, trying to control his thrashing as he attempted to strike again at the evil thing before us. Dumbfounded, I couldn't even open my mouth to ask why the man had reacted the way he did.

Carl appeared in the hallway and started hammering us with questions while Mr. Varble and I stood our ground at arm's length.

"What happened?! What's going on here?"

Sidney's barking echoed furiously in the corridor.

Never taking his eyes off me, Mr. Varble said, "Her dog tried to bite me."

"Only after you kicked him!" I shouted back, holding onto his stare with equal intensity. Sidney had quit struggling, but he continued to bark into the man's face.

Mr. Varble sneered at me and turned his head toward Carl. "I want that dog out of here."

Flustered, Carl's eyes batted nervously as he shook his head. "Now, wait a minute," he said, trying to calm us both. Looking at me, he asked again, "What happened?"

I looked directly at Carl and said in my calmest voice, "Sidney walked over to the doorway of his old apartment and that man kicked him."

Mr. Varble never countered my claim or tried to offer another explanation. He simply repeated, "I want that dog out of here."

Carl was obviously torn. I could see he believed me, but I also knew how desperate he was for the money his tenants provided. I thanked my lucky stars that he had never found out about Sidney's reaction to Lumberjack. Two such incidences, no matter how provoked this last one was, would surely have landed us on the street. Carl lowered his head while his right hand picked nervously at his scruffy tee shirt. "Okay," he finally said. "Mrs. Warner, could you possibly take Sidney out the back from now on?"

I wanted to stand my ground, but in fairness to Carl, I nodded agreement.

"And you, Mr. Varble." Carl avoided direct eye contact as he said, "I'm not sayin' you was wrong, but I've known Mrs. Warner a long time now, and in all her dealings with me, I've never known her to lie."

I could not stop the blood that rushed to my face.

Mr. Varble did not protest the implied accusation against him. He simply stepped back into his apartment, mumbled "I hate dogs," and slammed the door in our faces.

Carl looked at me and shrugged.

I lowered Sydney to the floor and let my shoulders sag. "I promise you, Carl. Sidney did nothing wrong."

"I believe you," Carl said in his quietest voice, perhaps not aware of how futile it was to whisper in such a place. "Don't you worry," he assured me. "I'm not throwin' you and Sid out for the likes of him." He thumbed at the closed door. "You and Sid are welcome here for the rest of your days, far as I'm concerned."

I know Carl meant his last statement as a comfort.

* * *

Sidney was in no mood to walk one Thursday morning. The oppressive summer heat had returned for one last stand against autumn, and all he could do was wander, listless, along the edge of the sidewalk next to the hotel. I stepped into the grass and tugged at the leash to encourage him. When that did not work, I picked him up bodily and deposited him a few feet into the grass. "Poop," I commanded in a quiet voice. He only managed to snap at a fly buzzing near his head.

When Sidney decided to lay down in the shade, I took my cue and sat on the grass beside him. I'd been picking at some wild violets for a while before I noticed a dark face staring from the shadows of our old apartment. Mr. Varble was watching us through the high window. I held his gaze for a very long time. When he became uncomfortable, or simply grew tired of standing, he moved back out of sight. I reached over and scratched behind Sidney's ears. "Let's go, buddy," I said, climbing to my feet. "I'll bring you out again later."

We wandered back through our private door. Sidney took his spot in front of the box fan, and I stood in the middle of the room staring at the cavernous hole that led to the bedroom. I don't know if it was Mr. Varble's treachery, Zoe's kindness, or Mystery Writer's query, but something broke the lock on my spirit.

"This is my home now," I exclaimed to Lumberjack's ghost. Sidney didn't even turn an eye in my direction.

I forced myself into the bedroom to rearrange furniture and put my spare things away in the drawers. I made an internal commitment to rent a shampooer and see how much of the blood stain I could remove from the carpet. After a couple of hours of vigorous polishing, I decided to take a break and cool off in the library.

Zoe was alone behind the desk. She smiled at me when I came through the doors.

"How are you?" I asked.

"Good," she said in a noncommittal way.

That answer was no longer enough. "How is the treatment going?"

Without moving a muscle, Zoe seemed to retreat from where she was sitting. It struck me then that her full head of hair no longer signaled health. It meant resignation. I tried to stifle the mercy that came pouring out, but to no avail.

"Zoe, I'm so so sorry. Is there nothing they can do? Is there anything I can do?" How arrogant, I realized after I'd asked the last question, as if my life had some bearing on hers. My selfish life. But Zoe had the answer.

"Just be my friend," she said. "I could use a good friend." She motioned for me to come behind the counter and sit with her a while. We talked mostly small talk. I asked about her family. She had no one to speak of. "The spinster librarian," she joked.

When she asked about my family, I hesitated. "I was married once."

"Well." She folded her hands in her lap and gave me an obscure smile. "Here we are then." After a brief moment of silence we both laughed hysterically. When we quieted enough to speak again, she said, "I cheated on a homework assignment in the seventh grade."

I smiled and countered, "I used to eat the candy in a store where I worked as a teenager."

Her eyes twinkled as she told me, "When I was twenty-four, I stole a highway caution sign. I felt so guilty, I returned it the next night."

She was giving me permission. Zoe would never ask me straight, but she wanted me to know that I had her confidence. It seemed so natural to say it.

"My name is not Mary Warner."

She didn't flinch. She didn't even lose her smile.

"And I'm not divorced."

Before I could say anything more, the spell was broken by two children who came racing through the double doors, heading for the young adult book section.

Zoe greeted them and then turned back to me. "I should get to work." She pulled a list from her work pile and laid it in front of her. "Come see me tomorrow before school gets out."

I said I would and then walked back to the hotel, all the while wondering how far I could trust her with the truth.

Inside the apartment, I found Sidney pacing the floor. There was evidence he had been sick. I hurried to put the harness on and managed to get him outside where he was sick again. He paced, almost running at times, and then he would stop to vomit. I felt sorry and irritated at the same time. He stopped moving long enough to have a terrible bout of diarrhea. At that point he simply laid down in the grass and started pulling at the tender green with his teeth.

"I'm so sorry, buddy." I offered to rub his head and neck, but he growled at me—something he'd never done before. "I'm sorry," I said again and pulled my hand away. He looked at me with the queerest expression, let out a yelp followed by several whimpers and then simply lay over on his side, panting. Shaking. Nothing I could do would coax him to his feet. I was afraid to pick him up.

I tied the leash to a nearby bush and ran to the front of the hotel.

"Carl, I need your help! It's Sidney. He's really sick. Could you drive us to a vet?" I led Carl out of the lobby and toward the lawn. Sidney lay where I'd left him.

"Can you get him up?"

I reached one hand for Sidney's muzzle and clamped his mouth while I ran my other hand under his chest to lift him. He screeched in pain, but I managed to gather him into my arms. Carl untangled the leash just as I looked up at the window of my old apartment to find Mr. Varble's wretched face staring back at us. He was smiling.

* * *

I am heartbroken to this day. How can I possibly express what Sidney meant to me at that point in my life. He was my companion, confidant, protector. He never questioned my integrity, and he never asked for more than I could give him. For a week, I mourned alone in my apartment. Carl would come by each morning to ask if there was anything he could do. I would send him away. I bawled like a baby, exhausting myself, only to start again the next day.

I found myself shooting daggerous stares toward my old apartment. Fortunately for Mr. Varble, we never managed to open our doors at the same time. He had poisoned Sidney, and I had absolutely no proof. Even if I had, I could never have accused him publicly.

I made myself get out of bed the following Friday. I showered and changed, and before I realized exactly where I was headed, I found myself walking into the library. Someone new stood behind the desk.

"Is Zoe here?"

She looked at me with an odd expression. "Are you family?"

"No," I said.

"Is there something I can help you with?"

"No," I repeated rather abruptly. "I came to see Zoe."

She took my rude response and returned it in kind. "Zoe no longer works here."

Still too dense or too grief-stricken to understand what she was not telling me, I started to ask why when the head librarian stepped out of the back office.

"Mary," she said, smiling at me. "How are you?"

"Not good," I complained. "I really wanted to speak to Zoe. When will she be back?"

Her smile lingered a little too long. "She's not coming back. She's in the hospital."

"No," I said reflexively. "She can't be. I need to see her."

I must have seemed pitiful to the two of them. Drab, sullen, selfish. When I finally came out of my stupor enough to think, I asked, "Where is she? Can I go see her?"

The librarian hesitated only a moment. "I'm sure Zoe would want you to know. She's at the university hospital in Iowa City." She leaned onto the desk and wrote something on a slip of paper. "These are her room and telephone numbers. I'm sure she'd appreciate a visit from you." It was less a statement than an appeal.

I thanked her and wandered back into the street. "What can I do with these?" I thought, staring at the numbers, but I knew I had to go. I had to tell her the whole truth.

Over the next two days, I borrowed Carl's phone to gather information on bus routes. When Monday arrived, I awoke early, still fighting the feeling that I should take Sidney for his early morning walk first thing.

I showered and pulled on my drab uniform of black slacks and casual top, and started my walk to the nearest motel. From there, I shuttled to the casino, the Des Moines bus station and along the stretch of Highway 80 that took me to Iowa City. It was eleven-thirty when a taxi picked me up for the final leg to the university hospital. I made a mental note, calculating how much of my precious resources would be spent on this trip, and just as quickly chastised myself for thinking that it mattered.

As I stepped through the rotating door and into the lobby, the crisp, October air gave way to a mix of odd medicinal smells that permeate every medical facility. In contrast, the lobby was full of people shopping, visiting, snacking on light lunches.

At the information desk, I asked for directions to Zoe's room. After a couple of false starts, I managed to find the correct wing of the correct floor. I hesitated outside her room. I glanced at my empty hands and felt ashamed that I had not brought a card. It would have been an empty gesture, but a gesture nonetheless. How could I have fallen so far from the compassionate, caring person I used to be? I no longer recognized anything honorable within me. And still I pushed forward into the room.

Zoe, a tiny woman to begin with, seemed insignificant amid the count-less machines, tubes and wires that traveled to and from her shrunken body. In just over a week, her face had pulled into her skull leaving large hollows under her cheekbones. Her thick short hair matted to her head. She saw me, and immediately, the corners of her mouth tipped up just a little.

"Come in, come in," she ordered with a weak gesture of her hand. She patted the bed and whispered, "Come sit here."

I walked to her bedside, careful not to touch anything attached to her or a monitor, and sat gingerly on the side of the mattress.

"I'm fine," she replied to my silent question. With a tiny shrug she added, "It's my lot in life this round." She drew in a deep breath to recover her voice and asked, "What's your name?"

"Rebecca," I said without hesitation. "Becca, to my friends."

"Becca." Zoe rolled the name over as if to inspect it for the truth. "That suits you better."

I dropped my eyes to my hands and fidgeted with their emptiness. After a long silence, I looked at her and said, "I'm so sorry you are going through this. I'm so sorry…" She reached for my hands to stop me.

"I've made my peace. I think it's time you made yours." She slipped her fingers into mine and gave a firm squeeze. "Tell me, Becca, what brought you here."

I couldn't stop myself. I told her everything from Dottie's misdeed and my complacency, to how I had deceived Carl. I laid out the story of Mystery Writer and recited word for word what I'd written in the letters, how I'd laid out the crime scene in detail.

"You cannot imagine what it was like," I said, "to wake from the struggle only to be suffocating in blackness." I was sorry as soon as I had said it. Zoe could imagine.

"Go on," she prompted.

I shuddered briefly, fighting the memory. "I ripped the trash bag away from my face and lay gasping under a layer of leaves and dirt," I told her. "For a while I couldn't remember my own name. I crawled out of the pit and hid behind the studio. I watched for hours as my husband worked to hide what he thought was a murder. At first I was only stunned, but then I grew angry. I tried to imagine what the police would do to him if I reported the assault." My eyes flared with a darkness that surprised even me. "He was good at talking people out of things. At worst, he would receive a shorter sentence than I was sure he deserved."

I stopped talking and looked at Zoe's serene expression. "Perhaps you can't understand this, but I could think of nothing greater than the hell I could heap upon him as a ghost." I turned away for a moment. "The truth," I said, turning back, "is that I was afraid to face him. Too cowardly to confront him with what he'd done. Too afraid I would forgive him. And so," I raised my hands into the air, "Becca vanished."

Zoe watched with pity in her eyes. "You saved yourself," she told me then. "There's nothing disgraceful in that." She looked tired, fighting to keep her eyes open.

"I'm sorry," I blurted out. "I'm wearing you down."

"Nonsense," she admonished. Again she grabbed my hand. "Thank you."

I couldn't hide my surprise. "For what?"

"For trusting me."

When I knew my time with her was over, I said, "Your turn to tell a secret."

A low moan escaped her throat. "I loved a married man once." She paused for effect. "And then he divorced me." Still she clung to humor. "I should rest now. I'll see you soon."

I leaned in to hug her frail shoulders. "Yes," I repeated. "See you soon."

We both knew we were lying.

* * *

I fell into a dark depression over the next two months. My limited existence became even more constrained as my reasons for escaping the hotel had now all disappeared. Carl kept a close eye, and when he realized that I had not been out of my apartment in over two weeks, he offered to buy groceries. I let him.

I heard him rattling plastic bags on his return from the store. He tapped lightly, and I pulled myself up from the couch to open the door.

"Here's yer things," he said, handing me two small sacks. "I put yer change in the one with the orange juice." When his right hand was free, he removed the cigarette from the corner of his mouth using the butt of his hand to cover a phlegmy cough. "You jus' let me know if yer needin' anything else."

I held the bags open and stared at the contents. Without looking up, I asked, "Do you want to come in for a moment?"

"Why, sure. You must be pretty lonely in here without Sidney."

I backed away to give him room to enter.

"I still can't believe someone would poison a innocent dog like that." He gravely shook his head and walked to one end of the couch.

I put the groceries away in the kitchen and returned to the overstuffed chair that Dottie had used only as a repository for magazines and newspapers. I turned from a vision of blood-soaked newsprint to the sight of Carl's smoking hand, shaking steadily as he pulled his cigarette to and from his lips. I sat quietly and watched the gray plumes create patterns in the air around his head. He looked uncomfortable, but I couldn't bring myself to start the conversation.

"So," he ventured after another thirty seconds had passed. "Did you want to git another dog? Ya know I wouldn't mind, if that's what you want."

"I don't know," I murmured. "I honestly haven't thought about it."

"Well, I wouldn't mind, ya know."

"Thank you. I'll let you know before I do."

After another minute of silence, Carl pulled forward on the seat. Before he could stand, I stopped him with a question. "Why were you in prison?"

He raised his eyebrows and relaxed back into the couch. "Most people are afraid to ask. Me, I don't mind talkin' about it. I made mistakes, but who hadn't?"

I nodded. "How bad was it?"

"Bad enough. I was on the edge, ya know. I'd git in fights, or git a little drunk now and then. I did a little petty thievin', but never got caught for that." He looked genuinely remorseful. "No, I got time for knockin' a fella so hard he lost an eye. I used to have a pretty bad temper."

I laughed out loud, but Carl didn't seem to take offense.

He continued. "I only did two 'n a half years the first time, but it hit me pretty bad. I was use to a hard bunch on the outside, but nothin' like what was living inside."

It seemed he'd been waiting, perhaps for years, to tell his story. I needed to spend some time outside myself, and so I listened.

He rambled on for another ten minutes, explaining the reasons why they kept sending him back into confinement. "That was when I finally figured out how dumb I was," he concluded. "I figured it was time to straighten up. Git something ligit goin'."

We were silent again, but this time neither one of us felt the need to rush through it.

"Remember you asked me about my money?" I said and watched him perk up with interest. "I won it from the casino."

"Well, I'll be damned," he said. "That's how I got the money for this place. Cost me sixty grand, and I've been losin' money ever since. Why the last assessment they said it was only worth forty-seven thousand dollars. And this being a historical building and all."

"I'm sorry," I told him. "I know how hard you work to keep it up."

"Well, I do what I can."

For a moment he looked uneasy, and then a resolve came over him. "I know things have been rough for ya the last couple a months, Dottie, but you shouldn't let things get you down like this." He seemed oblivious to the fact that he'd gotten my name wrong. "Take it from me. I know about this stuff."

Just as quickly as it began, his lecture was over. He slid to the front of the sofa again. "Well, I'd best get back to that work or things 'll fall apart for sure. I'll be firin' up the boiler in another two weeks." He stood up and looked for a place to get rid of his cigarette butt. Finding nowhere to drop it, he took it with him to the door. "It'd be best if you'd get another dog."

I nodded and said I would consider it.

Carl let himself out.

I realized that my entire life had been devoted to searching out people who would tell me what to do. My husband had been the consummate expert in what was right for me. I bowed to his will because I had no direction of my own. With no one to guide me, my last two years living in the hotel had simply been inertia at rest. How selfish of me to have laid that burden on others.

The flat light from the bare bulbs washed over Dottie's living room, and I noted the handful of past receipts written in Carl's illegible hand and made out to Mrs. Warner. Nothing here had ever been mine.

From Carl's private rooms off the lobby, I heard him coughing up his evening phlegm to make room for a little oxygen. I could picture the cigarette jerking in his right hand.

It was late when I finally opened my apartment door to the cavernous hallway. I stood staring at the number fourteen that graced the door to my old apartment and wondered if I had the nerve to pound on it until Mr. Varble was obliged to open it and meet my wrath. Instead, I turned toward the lobby. Finally, I knew what I needed to do. With some regret, I stepped out of the Hotel Toledo for the last time.

Chapter Four

It was perhaps the most frightening thing I'd ever done, leaving Toledo. Every other major change in my life had been forced upon me. This was my choice. All I knew for certain was that I had to escape the hotel and Carl and Dottie's cursed apartment. There was one additional thing to break free of, and I couldn't do it in Iowa.

The ticket master in Ottumwa explained the boarding process and motioned to the row of hard plastic chairs along the glassed wall of the train station.

"The Number Nine train is coming in late and will be the first to pull in. Don't get on the first train," he said firmly, fatherly. "About ten minutes after it leaves, the Number Six will pull in. It's waitin' out of town right now. You wanna get on the Number Six." He shooed me toward the chairs.

I sat two seats away from a young woman, perhaps college age, who seemed engrossed in a book. I tried to glance at the title in case it was something we had in common. A conversation starter. When it didn't look familiar, I let my eyes wander to the rest of the interior.

The 1970's architecture had been cared for only slightly better than Carl's hotel. Just a train depot at one time, the space now doubled at the bus station. Two bus passengers waited on the opposite wall and stared at us through the invisible barrier that separated the classes. One man wore everything he owned layered on as if the temperature was sub zero. The other man teased me with his eyes and his body language, threatening to slide across the room and strike up a conversation. He could sense my discomfort. I caught his smile just before I looked away. Lucky money was the only thing that put me on this side of the room.

A last-minute couple, tickets waving, raced in with their luggage and managed to catch the Number Nine. As quickly as the noise had settled into the corners again, the Number Six pulled in from the opposite direction. I followed the college girl and her cumbersome luggage into the night air. The echoing whispers inside the building were absorbed into the humid, small-city noise. A porter checked our destinations and sent us to separate train cars. I was sad to sever whatever imaginary connection I'd built with the young woman.

On the train, I turned left up the spiral staircase to the seating deck. There were two empty seats right behind the bulkhead, and I settled into the one nearest the window. With my purse tucked under my elbow, I waited for the train to deliver me back into the fire.

All night, the train struggled along the track, sometimes jerking to a stop for no apparent reason only to start rolling forward again without announcement. The low interior lights overwhelmed the moonlit landscapes, hiding everything but the mercury vapors standing sentry over the sleepy farmhouses. The passenger cars swayed precariously with the jointed rhythm of the rails. I felt a world apart from everything I'd known in my life. I wanted to ride trains forever.

It took nine hours for the previous two years to be erased. At four-thirty in the morning, I disembarked at the McCook depot in Nebraska. It was a relief to be the only one there.

A dim light shown from inside the station, so I wandered in to get my bearings. The building was much older and architecturally more inter-esting than the one in Ottumwa, but the inside was sterile, the ticket counter barred and locked. One table and a handful of scattered chairs barely broke the monotony of the room. The bathroom was clean enough, but there was no lock on the door. I remembered where I was and relaxed into the business at hand.

At the table, I pondered every conceivable outcome of my visit. I listened to my breathing echo through the cavernous room and wondered if anyone was still looking for me. Had anyone in this town ever known me enough to remember who I was? What would they do if they saw me? What would *he* do?

When dawn finally broke across the tracks, I stepped out of the station and turned toward the business district. Within a few blocks, I was puff-ing up a steep hill covered in middle-class bungalows. The terrain leveled on a high plateau, and soon I passed the small community college that helped to drive the town's economy.

"He taught here," I reminded myself. I had hated the school functions—him parading his eccentricities before his raptured students, academics speaking snob-ese to one another. Me, the mousy wife in the corner attending the punch bowl. I had never been intellectual enough to suit him. What I lacked in intellect he lacked in ambition. I supposed that made us even.

I passed the college and turned down what used to be a crumbling private drive. There were houses now, crowding the pasture behind them. Five new modest homes spilled into the tangled underbrush that had once separated us from the city limits. I passed the graveled driveways and wondered if anyone was watching this early-morning interloper. At the end of the pavement, I stopped near a stand of young black locust.

It was still early, perhaps only five-thirty or six. The morning was November cool, but the dry air never stirred. I studied the house and marveled at how little had changed, how it sat frozen in the same state of disrepair. No better, no worse than when I'd left it. The only things new were the swaths of eddied leaves strung across an unused patio surrounding a barbeque pit. My gravesite. I leaned into the small tree trunks and waited for something to happen.

He appeared in the window. He walked up from the shadow of the living room and stood drinking a morning cup of coffee. His hair was longer, to his shoulders, and hung in the same disheveled fashion that labeled him a non-conformist. He held his cup with both hands and watched a half dozen starlings play in the yard. He turned, responding to someone, and I saw him smile. I knew she would be young. Perhaps a graduate student, perhaps not. Of course she would be pretty. She stepped to the window and, from behind, threaded her arms under his. They stared out the window, and together they stared right through me. Drab and gray as the bark of the locust, I was truly a ghost.

When they disappeared into the shadows again, I sank to my knees. Hugging my purse into my belly, I leaned over, rocking and humming my torment. I was a broken woman again. He knew himself to be a murderer, and yet everything I'd done, everything I had not been for the last two years had served up no reprisals. My only achievement was to free him to build whatever life he chose. I was too humiliated to be angry.

I wanted to call to someone, conjure a name that would bring me comfort. I felt a phantom warmth against the side of my leg. "Sidney," I blurted, reaching into the leaves to stroke his fur.

The garage door to the studio lurched open, and I scrambled back into the brush. It wouldn't do for him to find me in this state—a pitiful specter.

He lit the furnace and prepared his tools for a morning of glass work. He checked his blowpipes, blocks and paddles in the same ritualistic way he'd done for years, sorted through his powders and sands, felt each texture a moment longer than necessary. It was his rite before he began casting the ingredients into the fire. Nothing about his life had changed.

I thought of Dottie and how she had murdered Lumberjack, dissecting his body to dispose of it. My husband was guilty of assault, but it was I who had committed this murder. In my quest for revenge, I had dissected my life into worthless pieces that could be tossed as easily into the fire.

I watched him for hours, turning, shaping, blowing life into inert sand. I wondered what had happened to my bowl. The bowl. Perhaps he had destroyed it, melted it back into innumerable other creations. For a moment, it mattered.

The sun reached midday. A number of new vases—vibrant and sensual—cooled in the annealer. The studio stood empty, heat billowing out the open door.

I got up from the ground and brushed the leaves from my pantlegs. Picking my way through the bushes, I moved to the street and turned away from my past. Through town, past the campus, past the cottages, without intent, I found myself in the train station again. The ticket counter was open.

"May I help you?"

I could return to safety—to the hotel and obscurity—or I could reincarnate from the ashes. There would always be that chance I'd be discovered, perhaps even prosecuted for something. But people endure prison.

"Ma'am," the ticket salesman repeated. "May I help you?"

Sidney was gone. The few belongings left in the hotel—clothes, dishes, television, a slow cooker—could be replaced for less than one of the bills I hid at the bottom of my purse. Everything I was stood passively in this one spot.

"How cliché," I finally said.

"Pardon?"

"Phoenix. Phoenix, Arizona."

"Baggage check?" he asked, looking at my feet.

"No," I said. "No more baggage."

BEHIND
THE MASK
BOOK TWO

*To the rogues and misfits
who make up my surrogate family
at The Nook.*

PROLOGUE

I should have been there—invisible me—watching your face as they dug up my grave site. I can imagine how the veins in your neck would have raised and throbbed as they often did when you clenched your jaw against some affront to your character. In the side yard—overgrown with neglect—you would have stood passively, anxiously, flanked by at least two uniformed officers who, earlier, had explained the anonymous tip.

"Yes, sir. We have a court order to dig up the patio."

"The patio?" you would have choked out, certain after five years that no one else would come looking. Even your mother-in-law had stopped calling.

How did you conceal the terror you must have felt once the heavy equipment had scattered the top layer of brick and finally cracked the concrete base? You would have held your breath—your heart bursting in your chest—as the gargantuan claw of the backhoe flipped the slab over. Your wide eyes would have followed the forensic team in scrubs and masks as they rushed to sift through the decayed leaves and dirt. And after they had thoroughly combed the ground with shovels, rakes, and gloved hands, I wish I could have been one of those masked minions—the one who anonymously walked up to you and addressed the officer in charge.

"Nothing," I would have said. "No sign of a body."

It has been five years, and now you know. I am alive.

Chapter One

Phoenix—oven hot and overcrowded—had been another in a long line of poor life choices except for one thing. The city stripped me of the notion that I could survive anonymously into old age on the money I had stashed. During the previous three years hidden in small-town Iowa—before fleeing to rise again from my self-inflicted exile—I failed to carefully calculate my finances. But the hotel in Toledo was at least cleaner and less forbidding than the roach-infested room I could afford to rent in the Central City district of Arizona's capital. I escaped the valley of the sun soon after a fellow tenant connected me with a document forger. The process left me unsettled, having to trust to the discretion of someone perhaps not so trustworthy.

I carefully examined my new "proof of life." There was that face—that unadorned characterless face that reminded me of a composite of every set of human features on the planet. I looked like everybody. And nobody. My new driver's license and Social Security card would give Becca "Mills" six years in Kansas. Six years to decide whether or not I would literally rise from the dead.

My mother had promised so much more for me. I even had my own song as a child. Of course, it had been recorded long before I was born and had nothing to do with me. A sweet melody with doting lyrics by

Carol Hall and sung by Barbra Streisand. My father said my mother sang the first two lines to me in the delivery room.

Jenny Rebecca, four minutes old, how do you like the world so far?

The original lyrics are "four *days* old," but Mom found ways to adjust them to the moment.

Jenny Rebecca, four days old, what a lucky lucky lucky lucky girl you are.

When Mom was very young, and still had Cinderella dreams, she decided that her first daughter would be named after the song she loved so much. She married young. My father, a kind man, was nine years her elder. They both wanted children, but something in their chemistry would not allow it. Not that they obsessed to the point of seeking medical attention. It would happen when it would happen.

And then it did. Three times in thirteen years. All three miscarried. Until me.

For you have swings to be swung on. Trees to be climbed up.

Mom was no Barbra Streisand, but she did have a lovely lilting voice.

Days to be young on. Toys you can wind up.

The grass, the sun, the pillows to cry on when a boy broke my heart. Ponies, slides. Dogs. And above all, dreams. Her dreams. It was as if the song became the blueprint for my life just so my mother could sing it to me.

My doting parents had not properly prepared themselves for my rebellious years.

"Jenny Rebecca, please, we need to talk about this."

"It's Becca! Just Becca!"

From the other side of the door, I could hear her whispers. "Jenny. Please."

And then my father died. At forty-six.

All the dreams, all of the aspirations my parents had tried to inspire in me burned to ash. Rebellion and anger turned to guilt. As my mother spiraled into a deep depression, I became the parent. Quiet. Attentive. Subservient.

Just what David Sante wanted in a wife. Until he didn't.

When I walked away from everything I had known, I had promised myself no more emotional baggage. But as I floundered in the Arizona heat, unable to find focus, I couldn't escape the fact that my life was in shambles.

David, however, had set aside my ghost and moved on. He believed his clever deception insured that his secret would never come to light, that his heinous crime could never come back to haunt him. With no evidence of foul play, he could milk sympathy as the abandoned husband while quietly celebrating his freedom. He no longer had to pander to a mousy wife, and I could no longer try to prod him out of his complacency.

But I had my own future to consider. I began to obsess over planting a seed of uncertainty, of possible discovery. I was considering how best to undermine his surety when I settled on the anonymous tip. If the authorities followed through—digging up the patio and finding nothing beneath it—only David would know what that truly meant.

I made the anonymous call from Arizona to the Nebraska State Patrol's division investigating missing persons. Terrified that the call would be traced, I packed my over-sized purse and a small tote and boarded a bus to Wichita, Kansas.

I landed in the cheapest motel I could find that also gave me quick access to a library. Though Wichita was considerably smaller than Phoenix, this was only a layover until I knew how David would react. I spent the next few days tracking him on social media. It was easy to fake an Instagram account and follow his career. His social life.

Predictably, his posts played into the stereotype of a *big fish* art professor in a *small pond* college town—erudite, smug, nonconformist. He shared images of his art to the accolades of his puerile audience. His student followers—mostly women—offered him praise. Some offered much more. He responded to his adoring base as though his work held as lofty a status as a Chihuly or a Littleton. And then, just four days into my watch, his posts stopped.

The first indication that he had truly been shaken was the announcement on the McCook Community College website advertising to fill a vacant position. "Wanted. Adjunct Faculty Art Professor." It was possible he chose to leave, but it was equally possible that the renewed stain of suspicion over my disappearance made the campus administration uneasy. Either way, I wanted to know where he would land. I kept a vigil. And waited.

* * *

Baker University welcomed David with a great deal of fanfare. The new darling of the art department at a small but highly-respected institution. *Introducing David Sante, Adjunct Professor of Art.* The announcement touted Professor Sante's Master of Fine Arts and his status as a PhD candidate. A *candidate.* He had played up the ABD portion of his education for years—*All But Dissertation.*

"All but determined to finish it," I thought. I laughed out loud as I remembered what we had argued about the night he struck me. Dragged me to the side yard. Buried me.

David would not be in his new classrooms until August. That gave me four months to think and to plan. I checked out of the motel and took connecting buses to Lawrence—home to the University of Kansas. The town was just shy of a hundred thousand residents and had a large number of rentals, but those I could afford were merely rooms in shared apartments or houses, or they were in no better condition than what I'd suffered through in Phoenix. I appreciated the collage town vibe, but I did not fancy a roommate—especially a college student less than half my age. I continued to scour online for an available living space in the bustling city that would give me some distance and more anonymity than living in the small community that surrounded the Baker University campus. Then I realized that, without a car, the safer distance of fifteen miles might as well have been fifteen hundred. I turned my focus to Baldwin. That would certainly be a daring move—planting myself directly in his path. But the more I thought about it, the more I realized that living in the same town, small as it was, would provide me the best opportunity to observe him and, perhaps, reclaim my life once and for all. I clicked on a site for Baldwin rentals and found the perfect property.

* * *

The apartment was small. A three-hundred square foot studio, unfurnished. The building—as old as the historic hotel that had hidden me away for three years in Iowa—had been maintained in better condition. A large picture window in the south wall of the main living space and a double window in the kitchen area let the bright southern sun flood the room with energy and warmth. A thin set of sheers over the picture window provided little privacy, but the second-floor apartment faced a stand of trees across the street. I was not concerned about prying eyes. The view was invigorating. Fresh and green. Open to the sky.

The living area elled to the right to allow for a spacious kitchenette with new cabinets, but the light-oak eighties finish seemed incongruous with the white vintage woodwork in the rest of the room. A door in the north wall led to an over-sized bathroom with a walk-in shower. I turned on the hot water in the sink and smiled when I saw steam rising from the basin. Reliable hot water was more luxury than I had had in five years. The rent matched what I had paid in Iowa, but here I was expected to pick up the tab for electricity. Still, temporary as it was, the apartment checked off my every need.

There were three apartments on the floor above the street-level dance studio. Mine was isolated at the back of the building—no common wall with anyone else. Unless I met them on the stairs, I would not have to concern myself with the neighbors.

The space was larger than I needed—a glaring reminder that I owned nothing to fill the room. I made a list of the bare necessities and hoped to find most the following weekend in the nearby neighborhoods during the annual citywide garage sale I had seen advertised. I was sure to find a mattress, perhaps even a bed frame. No sofa. One overstuffed chair would do. A small kitchen table with two chairs, perhaps, and a dresser would round out the furnishings.

My landlady, Stacy—who also taught dance classes in the business below—copied my driver's license for her records, but as long as I paid my rent and made no trouble, I could not imagine she would investigate its legitimacy. May was coming to a close, and she offered to have one of the many used air conditioners now lining the upstairs hallway installed before the June heat set in. I declined. Though I had not experienced the Eastern Kansas humidity yet, I could not imagine it would be worse than two summers in a sweltering concrete box in Phoenix. I preferred not to spend the extra money.

"Let me know if you change your mind," she said, handing me the key. She walked down the twenty-seven steps that led to the door opening onto High Street.

Once alone, I stood in the middle of the floor and studied the room with its ten-foot ceilings, original pine floors, and thick carved moldings. Accenting the opening into the kitchen, the landlord or a past tenant had added two decorative corbels at the ceiling. The character of the space tugged at my creative side.

I had been an artist, once upon a time. That was how David and I met, as art majors at a state university. But years of letting him take center stage—of not wanting to compete for praise—dampened my creative spirit, sending me into the shadows. I wondered how much of the original spark was left and whether I could rekindle it. The thought of decorating the apartment appealed to me, but before I let my imagination run wild, I considered the fact that it might be a waste of my resources. I didn't know how long I would actually be here. Much of that depended on David.

Feeling secure in my surroundings, I pulled up the lining at the bottom of my purse and laid out the bundles of cash I had stored there. On the kitchen counter, I stacked the hundreds, twenties, tens, and fives into separate piles. In a community like Baldwin, it no longer felt important to keep the cache tucked under my arm everywhere I went. Perhaps I would find a smaller purse to carry only my day-to-day needs. After making a mental note of the tally, I placed the bundles on a shelf in one of the walk-in closets.

Outside the apartment, I walked the half a block to the corner of the picturesque downtown. Each street corner of the three-block business district sported lovely hanging baskets of petunias beneath gracefully arched poles that would flood the streets below with golden light once the sun went down. Wide sidewalks flanked streets bricked with ancient pavers worn smooth, first by horse-drawn carriages and then by more modern conveyances. To my right was City Hall—a sturdy building not quite as old as the town itself. Diagonally across from where I stood, was the oldest bank in town—a family-owned institution that dated back to the community's founding. With my fabricated papers, I considered opening a checking account, but quickly thought better of it. The bank would more easily uncover my forgeries.

Looking east, I counted a number of businesses along the south side of High Street. A block away stood the town library. On the north, the community maintained a lovely flower garden next to an historic red brick lumberyard that had been converted into an art center. I filed that information away for later.

I turned north, walking by the front entrance to the dance studio, and passed a number of other businesses and restaurants. The wide sidewalk appeared new and well kept, inlaid with a center strip of bricks that matched the brick-paved streets. At the north end of the block stood a hundred-year-old house, now a bookstore, bar and coffee shop. *The Nook.* I considered stopping in, but moved on past and crossed Grove street, then turned right to cross Eighth. At the corner of the university campus, two octagon stone columns served as a gateway to academia. It seemed safe enough—too soon for David to be wandering about—so I breathed in the warming spring air and walked on ahead.

Baker campus radiated charm. Covering six small-town blocks, the buildings lining the perimeter surrounded a quad that resembled a well-groomed park. In the center, what appeared to be an artificial spring rose from a man-made rock formation and trickled downhill toward an arched stone bridge. Beneath the bridge, the stream flowed into a pond that collected the water and returned it uphill to the spring. I walked along the shallow creek, stopping on occasion to watch the first of the dragon-flies hover, dart, light on the stray blades of grass growing tall along the stream's edge. From the bridge, I looked down at the rotting leaves just under the water's surface where a thousand fresh tadpoles vied for the safest position as a small number of captive-gone-wild goldfish picked them off. Some student—leaving for the semester or the end of school, perhaps—must have failed to find a new home for the fish. I envied them the fact that their world had expanded ten thousand fold. Yet they had now become the target of even larger predators that would not hesitate to snatch their new-found freedom from them.

Summer classes had not yet started, so the quad was quiet except for an older couple—townies, I assumed—walking the oval path around the green space. My eye followed as they walked past the stone buildings that reflected the hundred and fifty year history of the campus. What appeared to be the oldest, a three-story sandstone structure with high arched windows and a bell tower, drew me over. Beneath the mansard roof, a number of decorative corbels highlighted the Second Empire architectural style common in the mid 1800s. Nervous, I climbed the steps to an aged set of green double doors and peered through the wavy glass panes. Pulling at the handle, I was surprised when the door swung open. I stepped inside.

The large center hall led to a far room with the name *Holt-Russell Gallery* over a more modern set of doors. I walked up to them, currently locked, and peeked through the narrow vertical windows. The room sat empty, waiting for the first exhibit of the fall semester. On the north wall inside the gallery, another door led to what appeared to be an office. The campus had wasted no time engraving *David Sante* on the nameplate beside the door. I realized that this would be his academic home once his tenure began.

I stepped back toward the building's entrance and looked through a glass wall into a room set with period furniture and resembling a stately colonial-era living room. Curiosity drew me in. The simple but elegant Queen Anne sofas and chairs appeared ready to host a formal tea if not a serious discussion between campus administrators. On the wall beside an ornate fireplace, I spotted the image of Abraham Lincoln. Studying the surrounding frames, I learned that Lincoln had donated a hundred dollars in 1858—the equivalent of over $3000—to the construction of the building, Parmenter Hall.

"Quite the claim to fame," I said aloud.

"Isn't it, though?" a male voice behind me asked.

When I caught my breath, I turned to face a short, lean older man dressed in a security uniform. He was smiling, so I forced my shoulders to relax. "Hi. I was just looking around. I hope that's okay."

"Certainly," he said. "We get a lot of visitors in the summer wanting to check out the campus. New students and their parents."

I read his name tag and then let my eyes wander around the rest of the room.

"You have a kid going here?" he asked.

"Oh. No. I just moved to town and thought the campus was so beautiful. I was just looking," I said again.

He turned and started across the hall toward a room I now realized was the campus security office. Before he disappeared, he turned back and said, "If you haven't seen it yet, you will want to visit the Osborne Chapel. It's just across the way." He pointed to the far side of the quad. "Should be unlocked."

I thanked him and left. With my heart racing, I walked back toward the downtown and decided to duck into The Nook to catch my breath.

The building that housed the bookstore was another period gem, still adorned with its original gingerbread highlighted in contrasting colors. It had been a home of some stature in the late 1800s—perhaps for someone connected to the university. At least one structural addition to the front of the building turned the house into a commercial enterprise that still added an abundance of charm to the downtown business district. The front lawn, between the structure and the sidewalk, had been concreted over and set with a number of tables and chairs. No one was about, so I walked up the steps and pulled the door open.

"Welcome to The Nook!" a vibrant voice said in greeting. "What brings you in today?"

Unnerved for the second time, I fought the urge to run.

"I just moved to town," I said, repeating my standard line. "I'm just looking around."

"Great. If you haven't been in before, then know that we're a bookstore, coffee shop, and full service bar. Look around, and let me know if you need any help."

I thanked her and moved farther into the building. The new-book section on the south side of the store held a collection of recent titles, time-honored classics, and local hand-made products. At the back end of the room, the owner had turned an old marble-topped soda fountain into a full-service bar. It created a sense of welcome not common in other bars.

At the center of the building sat a coffee shop—Jitters—in a room with windows and doors that paid homage to the original exterior of the house. Leaded glass and heavy moldings invited coffee lovers into the cozy space to order lattes and scones or the lunch special of the week. On this particular day, the aroma of fresh biscuits permeated the air.

The north side of the shop offered a play area beneath the stacks of children's books. Toys and a child-sized table and chairs were cordoned off by a charming picket fence that invited children to spend time while their parents browsed. Beyond that space, the left wall offered sixty percent off used books. Opposite those shelves, the owner had arranged a comfortable seating area—less like a business and more like a home.

After reading through the titles in the used books section, I found a paperback for a discounted price and made my purchase.

"I'm Niki," the woman said, handing me the book.

"Becca. I'm sure I'll be back."

I took the book to my apartment and sat on the bare wooden floor. The late May weather still held a chill, so I stretched, catlike, beneath a sunbeam to soak it in. Flipping the pages, I tried to concentrate on the novel, but kept thinking back to David's nameplate on his new office door. Moving to Baldwin could turn out to be one more bad decision in my life.

"No," I said to the hollow space. "I'm not the one who buried a body."

As the earlier adrenaline began to subside, I laid down on the floor and let the weariness wash over me.

Chapter Two

I developed a habit for The Nook over the next week. Niki offered the lounge area for me to read whatever I wanted off of the used bookshelf. The soft couches or the wingback chair helped relieve the aches accumulated from my bare floors, and Niki's two part-time employees respectfully wandered past without paying me much mind.

The Friday after I'd moved into my apartment, I headed south down Eighth Street in the hopes of scoring a good deal on furniture for my humble living space. At one particularly fruitful address, I bought a twin bed and headboard, and a small kitchen table with three chairs—not that I needed three. I paid the modest fee and a bit extra for the service of having them delivered up the stairs. Across the street and two blocks down, I found a small gray club chair and matching ottoman. Again, the owner helped muscle them up the twenty-seven steps.

For the rest of the day, I casually walked the area south of downtown and learned the alphabetical east-west street names and those numbered north and south. I lived at Eighth and High. The Nook stood on Eighth and Grove. The grocery store was eight blocks north on Ames Street—a pleasant enough walk if the weather was nice. In Phoenix, I would never have ventured so far from my room without the escort of a taxi driver, but in Baldwin, I felt unafraid strolling the streets that seemed grounded in some kinder era.

Sunday morning, I took advantage of the half-off sales to purchase a few basic items for the kitchen. Over the two days, I had spent less than a hundred dollars which included a week's worth of food. Not enough to worry me. But I knew, at some point, that the money I had cached to carry me into old age would run low. Unless, of course, some malady took me first. Hopefully, someone in town would hire me without references.

It had been decades since I had held any type of job. As the wife of a college professor, my duties involved volunteering to hostess events at our home or at school, and community programs for the college. Of course, it mattered very little now, even if I had had a job to reference. I could not even mention my Bachelor of Arts degree. Then I thought of The Nook.

In the days ahead, I not only spent time at The Nook, but I began to engage Niki in conversation. She was easy to talk to—outgoing and curious—though I only approached her when she was alone. And when she asked about my life, I had to be careful how I responded. If I could befriend her, gain her trust, perhaps she would forgo the background check. I could not imagine a better way to supplement my income than with work near to my heart. Since connecting with Zoe, the librarian in Toledo, Iowa, literature had become a passion. Fine art could be again. I was beginning to suspect that Baldwin had strong communities in both.

June warmed into the mid-eighties. Fortunately, the apartment had north and south windows that let in a lovely cross breeze, but midday, I did feel the moist air closing in. On cool nights, cicadas crooned me to sleep, and the conversations between early-morning walkers woke me before sunrise. I fell into a comfortable rhythm, relaxing more than I had for more years than I could count. Certainly since after I had married.

I thought I would miss the television that used to mask the pain when I lived in constant fear and isolation. The fear had been replaced by the adrenaline rush of temerity and anticipation. And thanks to Niki, the isolation had begun to lift.

Through the month of July, I considered asking my landlady to install the air conditioner, but I still had no additional income. Instead, I spent more time at the bookstore. Niki didn't seem to mind my trespassing, and she kept me informed on any newly-released novel that might be worth my time. Some books carried me into magical worlds or simpler times. Others reminded me of my own life—tragic and complicated. When I began to question whether I related more to the protagonist or the antagonist, I would put the book back on the shelf and move on. Every two or three days, I traded The Nook for the library, using their computers to track David's movements.

In the quiet hours at home, I often thought of Zoe. I had never properly grieved for her. She may have been the truest friend I had ever had and yet, for a long time after she died, I held the abandonment against her. As if it was her fault. The cancer. On those nights, sleep evaded me until late in the morning. It was Zoe who had opened the world of literature to me. And Zoe who had created a space safe enough I could start processing my pain. She deserved better than what I had given her at the time.

* * *

Of the two part-time employees at the bookstore, Lauren and I seemed to have the most in common. A psychology major, she had just finished her freshman year at Baker. She was as reserved as I was, but when she engaged with the customers over a book, her eyes lit up. All were impressed with her knowledge and the fact that her Goodreads profile indicated she'd read over three hundred books in her scant nineteen years. Because I kept to myself, most of what I did learn about her came from eavesdropping on her conversations with Madi.

Madi was in her senior year, but because of a sports injury, she was not eligible to graduate quite yet. When she did, her degrees would be in sports administration and business. Less interested in the book side of the store, she tended bar a couple of evenings a week. As reserved as Lauren was, Madi was on the opposite end of the spectrum. Outgoing, opinionated, outwardly confident.

The Nook's bar had its regulars.

Don—the native Texan, a Sam Elliot look-alike, sheet metal man, soon to retire. He drank Captain Morgan and Coke, and had the most beautiful head of silver hair. Gregarious, he read the classics and Stephan King, and did yoga at the studio next door. His philosophy: "If you're in a difficult situation, the first time you're polite. The second time, you're courteous. The third time," he'd make a fist and growl, "you get mean!"

Deb—the flower lady who sprinkled her volunteer time over several organizations. She traded the occasional vodka tonic for her gardening expertise and kept the patio blooming from spring through fall.

Jim—the guitar-playing fireman, retired. He preferred Merlot but never more than two glasses. He had moved away from Baldwin, but the community still held a soft spot in his heart. He returned each Saturday, and always the first Monday of the month for the Boozie Book Club.

Liz—the financial adviser who worked a few doors down the street and played on Niki's volleyball team. Slender and beautiful, she stopped in over lunch to visit and vent the latest frustration over the man who refused to give her a divorce.

Casey—a fourth-grade teacher at the local elementary school. Married to Jake, a banker. She liked The Nook's signature drink, the Bookworm, and he preferred a classic screwdriver. Casey was, herself, a bookworm.

And then there was Chris—the self-confessed compulsive liar. Nobody knew quite what to do with him. I listened in on his rants about religion, his disparaging remarks about the *youth today*—not that he was much older—and his contrived story about the CIA recruiting him as a result of his time as an Abercrombie & Fitch model. One day he would talk about his life as a cowboy. Another, he worked security. And still another, he would brag about working undercover to help girls escape sex trafficking. Delusions of grandeur.

"That's where they get all of their recruits from," he said one night. "Abercrombie & Fitch."

"Where who gets their recruits?"

"The CIA."

I kept my mouth shut, aware that my real life was far more subversive than his fantasies might ever be.

"If you actually worked for the CIA," Don said, "shouldn't you be keeping that to yourself?"

"Well, I trust you."

"Maybe you shouldn't," Jim said, not holding back his disdain.

Don looked my direction. "Assholeo," he said, winking.

I smiled. Despite some of their idiosyncrasies, this group of misfits began to feel more like family than my own blood.

The building was a character in itself. One evening, Niki shared a story about the book club which had gathered the night before. The women were drinking wine and discussing their latest read when a random book—*The Wine Merchant's Daughter*—fell from one of the top shelves and startled them all. As I listened to Niki's retelling, a book on a lower shelf behind where I sat tumbled to the floor—seemingly on its own. We eyed each other.

"Okay, now that's just super creepy," Niki said as I walked over to return the book to the shelf. "What's the title of that one?"

"*Paris the Novel.*" I secured it in place and walked back to the bar.

"Have you ever been to Paris?"

I climbed back on the stool and nodded. "Yes, in high school. I did a study-abroad program one summer."

"Well, that's too coincidental, don't you think?"

Before I could agree with her, *Paris the Novel* hit the floor again. We both stared dumbly at the tome.

"I suppose this means I have to buy it," I said, smiling. "Perhaps you should advertise the bookstore as *haunted*. Spend time here, and the store will tell you what you should read." It felt good to genuinely laugh again.

* * *

In early August, I approached Niki about working at the store. I tried to sound casual about the request, as if I didn't need the work.

"With both Lauren and Madi trying to get hours in over the summer, I can't use you at the moment," she said, "but when Baker starts back up, their hours here will be limited. I certainly could use you then."

I nodded and said I would appreciate being considered.

I continued to read whatever I could get my hands on at the store. Some books I purchased, some I read and returned to the shelves. In my spare apartment, the stack of used books began to mount, filling a corner near the door. A bed, a table and chairs, and a stack of books. These were my first possessions—other than my meager wardrobe—since leaving Nebraska.

There were many things I'd left behind, most of them in the house David had now listed with a Realtor. I questioned whether or not the sale would be legal since my name was still on the deed, but a little research at the library showed that it was possible. David must have taken his case to court. With a judgment in his favor, he was permitted the sale, but he would be required to put half of the proceeds in trust just in case I showed up in another fifteen years. My name had never been on the mortgage. That simplified things for him.

On the Realtor's website, I scrolled through the online photos showcasing a modest fifties ranch with a freshly-painted exterior and manicured lawn. The patio had been repaired. His glass stock, furnace and cooling kilns were gone from the two-car garage now patiently waiting for an SUV and a lawnmower.

Inside, the bedrooms were staged with generic furnishings. All of his artwork had been removed from the walls and replaced with a couple of simple landscapes over contemporary headboards. Prints, most likely. Not his taste or mine. The bright jewel-toned walls he'd agonized over before getting them just right had been painted a bland ecru. The kitchen looked the same as it had the last time I prepared a meal on the laminate counter tops that should have been replaced two decades earlier. A dried flower arrangement—the only organic shape in the dining room—sat centered on a square oak table. The hand-blown glass chandelier David had labored over for weeks had been traded out for a basic square fixture that looked too small for the room. He must have gutted anything of value to move with him. Or, more likely, to sell.

I imagined that he had turned some of my personal things over to my mother. I cared for nothing of my old life, but Mother would have begged for anything to keep my memory alive—to keep the heartache fresh.

In the online photos, the only personal item left in the house appeared to be a custom art piece—a glass bowl on the coffee table in front of the living room sofa. *The* glass bowl. My bowl.

"Why," I thought, "would he leave that in the house?" I shuddered.

I logged out of the computer and quickly left the library. On the walk back to my apartment, I kept reliving the night he had crafted the bowl with its delicate fingers lifting gracefully off the edges of a clear oval base. Bits of vibrant color swirled through each crystal strand giving the impression that something had just entered the water and thrown up shards of sea glass. The visual representation of an impact brought a phantom pain to my brow. Remembered pain. I could still feel the blood dripping into my eye from the blow of the paperweight that, after he thought I was dead and buried, he had returned to the fires to cleanse it of evidence. The murder weapon was now fused into his most stunning piece of art. Did he leave it there on the table just for show, or did he truly intend to abandon it? Perhaps it seemed too risky to keep. I wondered why he simply did not melt it down again.

Chapter Three

Niki trained me on the registers. "It's, like, so easy. Ten minutes and you'll have it down."

She soon discovered that I had an aptitude for communicating about the books I had been reading. Before long, many of the customers began coming to me with questions. I read many of the new releases and all of the book club picks so I could recommend a work or join the conversations. I didn't feel comfortable in the lead position during book club, but I could certainly add context and the occasional insight. Though I legally could serve alcohol, I had no talent for mixing drinks. I could, however, tend the bar in a pinch if everyone else was busy.

Classes had not started yet, but many of the student athletes moved in early to begin practice. One evening, three Baker seniors came in to celebrate the beginning of their final year as undergraduates. They settled at the bar and ordered shots of tequila.

After checking their IDs, I asked, "What are you guys studying?"

They looked at each other and then me. "You tell us," one of them said.

I had already overheard the fact that each played for one of the teams—soccer, football, and track and field. Knowing Madi's major, I took a wild guess and pointed at the first student.

"Sports Administration."

His eyes grew wide. "How did you know?"

I shrugged and smiled at the fact that it was the most obvious guess for anyone playing college sports.

The third student puffed up a bit and said, "Ok, do me. Do me now."

Not wanting to repeat myself, I went with the next most obvious option. "Business."

All three jaws dropped.

"How did you do that?" he asked.

"Don't you know?" I leaned into the bar. "I'm psychic."

I guessed wrong and killed the mystique with the third student, but we had formed a bond by then. They insisted on buying me shots for the next two rounds.

Many of the returning students knew Madi and would frequent the bar in the evenings to talk about schedules and who taught what—or, most often, who was dating whom. As I realized that the professors would be in the classroom soon, I started combing through the public notices for real estate sales. I wondered if David would buy or simply rent. Without tenure, or at least an associate position, renting seemed like the safest choice for him.

From Madi and her friends, I learned that a number of professors and Baker employees lived in Lawrence and drove to Baldwin. If that was David's choice, it would be much less likely I would run into him here.

Even so, it was inevitable in so small a town that we would cross paths sooner than later. But I wanted to be the one in control of that moment.

As my paycheck increased, I spent less of the money I had stashed. I seldom used it for anything beyond a portion of my rent. That freed up my finances to start buying supplies I had not purchased in a very long time. I bought pads and pencils from the Baker bookstore and started practicing my sketching—something I hadn't done in years. Sometimes I would draw from memory. Other times I would sit on one of the downtown benches and sketch the businesses along Eighth and High, or foliage from the small park across the street.

One afternoon, I wandered into the Lumberyard Arts Center. A bubbly woman, thin and stylishly dressed, greeted me.

"Hi. Welcome to the art center."

I nodded at her and then looked up at the fascinating original architecture of the center hall. "Wow," I said before I could stop myself. "This is an amazing building."

"Isn't it? We love it. So you haven't been in before?"

I admitted I hadn't. Jeanette showed me around the building—the classrooms, the boutique, the gallery space. "You're carrying a sketchbook," she said. "Are you an artist?"

I lowered my eyes. "It's been a long while. I'm just getting back into it."

She smiled brightly. "You should come to our Thursday afternoon Open Art. It's free, and you can meet some of the other artists in town."

As tempting as it was, I hesitated. I told her I would consider it.

She directed me to the guest book and asked that I sign. When I picked up the pen, I thought back to the library in Toledo where I'd used the alias of *Mary Warner*. I was truly a nobody then. I started to write *Becca Sante*, but quickly caught myself. *Mills* would do for now.

After spending more time looking at the exhibit in the gallery room, I walked back into the August heat and across the street to my apartment. Before I knew what inspired me, I was sketching a still life. In it, I centered a bowl with strands of glass reaching upward. I flipped the paper and started again, but my mind kept spilling the same image onto the page. Those strands—those fingers of glass—seemed as though they wanted to free themselves from the base. To free me. The more I sketched, the more precise the drawings became. But the drawings were not enough.

I made another trip to the campus bookstore and bought an array of watercolor supplies. Days passed, and the number of attempted works began to litter the floor of my studio. When I had exhausted nearly the entire pad of watercolor paper, I finally achieved what I had intended. David had executed his most stunning work of art in the bowl that held his secret. I had executed my most stunning work of art in the painting that finally set me free.

"You cannot hold me back any longer," I said, pulling the completed painting off of the pad. "I will own you soon enough."

* * *

I am a bibliophile. Certifiable. Not only had I unleashed the reader in me, but I discovered that the artistic side I had buried for decades had been living its own life—latent, secretive, fermenting. Free for the first time to pursue both of my passions, I stocked up on books and art supplies.

As a child, my mother had discouraged my art, only allowing for *pretty* pictures that she could show off to her friends.

94

"That's such a beautiful flower!"

"How lifelike!"

"Do you think you could draw my granddaughter?"

"Yes, but she'll never be able to make a living at it," my mother always countered.

When I branched into a subject or style that pushed expected boundaries, Mother's response was, "That's nice, honey, but…." Always, she tried to redirect my efforts into something milquetoast—safe and unemotional. If she could not explain it to her friends, she wanted no part of my creative endeavors. Too much controversy in my work might tarnish my *saleability*, might interfere with a women's most important reason to exist—being a good wife and mother.

As I began to explore new artistic processes, I had to push past the inner voice conditioned to hold me back. A sadness took root, less for me than for my mother. I realized that her life had been bound by her own programming, her inability to confront her own cowardice. She had been groomed to be the model wife—a support system for a successful husband. When my father died, she floundered for years, trying to give meaning to her existence. She settled on grooming me in her image. That became her sole purpose. She succeeded. To a point.

When David and I first met, he loved that we had art in common as long as he could be the pedagogue and I the subordinate. He was happy letting me pursue my art degree. Once we were married, and I surrendered my goal of teaching to support his career choices, he became more and more critical of my style. Soon, I was painting those pretty pictures my mother's friends loved so well. I grew to despise not just the paintings, but my inability to communicate what was in my heart. Pretty pictures became unfinished projects that degraded into incomplete sketches and finally ideas that never came to fruition.

David certainly had talent. But, over the years, his work took on a predictive quality that often mimicked the masters of his craft. I stopped sharing my own inspiration after seeing those ideas frequently pop up in his pieces or in those of his students. He would never admit, even to himself, that he was plagiarizing.

Now free of both my husband and my mother, I was desperate to break the lock, so one Thursday afternoon, I took Jeanette's advice and showed up at the art center. A half-dozen women and one gentleman had claimed their places around the tables in the classroom. Most were painting in watercolor—a medium I felt comfortable with. I poked my head into the room and waited for someone to look up.

"Hi there," a woman said. "Come to paint with us?"

I shrugged and stepped through the door. "I'm just looking around," I said, cringing at the worn out line. A chorus of welcomes rose from the tables, and I realized it would be rude to simply walk away. I sat at an empty spot and responded as obliquely as possible to their questions.

"I'm Sandy," said one of the painters. She went around the room. "This is Roma, Sharron, Robbie, Neal, Susan, Kathy. We have others that come and go."

"Nice to meet you. I'm Becca."

After a while, they returned to their various paintings and to the conversations that had started long before I arrived.

"Are you an artist?" Roma asked, taking a break from her Caribbean landscape.

I started to shake my head, but that would have been the professor's wife. Instead, I looked her in the eye and said, "Yes. I am."

"Great! We love new blood."

"You must be new to Baldwin."

"Where are you from?"

There were many answers to that question. "Phoenix," I said.

"What brings you to town?"

I hesitated longer than was comfortable.

"No matter," Sandy finally said.

The others worked through the three-hour session on whatever projects had inspired them. I promised to bring my paints the next week, and to follow the group to the Mexican restaurant afterward.

"It's tradition!"

"We call it 'extended ed'. Everyone goes for margaritas!"

I spent a few more minutes soaking up their generous smiles. That evening, I sat at my kitchen table and worked through some preliminary sketches of the flowers across the street. "Milquetoast," I grumbled. "Go away, Mother." I flung the pages to the floor and started running my pencil in random swipes across a new page. Before long, I had created a dark abstract that resembled some unrecognizable animal screaming.

* * *

In mid-September, I opened The Nook and greeted a young woman waiting to browse. After a few minutes in the store, she picked up a new release—a psychological thriller—and brought it to the front desk.

"Are you a Baker student?" I asked.

She laughed a trilling laugh and rolled her eyes. "Heavens no. I just moved here with my fiancé. He's a Baker professor."

As I checked her out at the register, she asked, "Do I know you?"

Studying her more carefully, I tried to remember everyone I had met since moving to town. She was medium height, young, blonde, and very attractive.

"I'm sure I've seen you before," she insisted. "Have you ever been to McCook, Nebraska?"

I froze, trying to control my expression. After what seemed like an eternity, I managed to mumble, "No. I've never been to the state."

She eyed me curiously and then said, "Well, you certainly have a twin somewhere."

After she left, I moved into the lounge area and sank into one of the overstuffed chairs. Surely, it couldn't be her, I thought. I tried to recall the woman I had seen in the window the morning I dared return to the scene of my husband's crime. I barely saw her face, but she had the right build, the right hair. The right vacuous personality that would appeal to David. What did he tell her? That I was missing? Dead? Did he even tell her he was married? Unless he had removed all of my photos from the walls and shelves, she would have seen my face a dozen times over. She would have been there when the authorities investigated the patio. How could she not be suspicious? David could be very persuasive, that I knew, but the fact that she had followed him from McCook to Baldwin meant she was either very trusting or very naive.

There was a sudden thump as another book threw itself to the floor. I calmed my heart rate and walked over to place it back where it belonged. Glancing at the title, I laughed and read out loud, "*Gone Girl.* Of course."

I went back to the register and looked at the name on the receipt. Lena Love. "How contrived," I said and caught a laugh in my throat. There it was again—that petty judgment I had cultivated over the years. Another trait I had inherited from my mother.

The store was quiet the rest of the morning. I checked off the daily duties and then curled up in a chair to read a new arrival. After a few false starts, I put the book back on the shelf.

Don, dressed in his usual loose tee with the sleeves cut out, wandered in after lunch. "Hey, darlin'!" His booming voice echoed through the quiet of the store. He carried a book he had finished and went to the shelves to exchange it for something else. "Have you read this one?" he asked, holding up a crime novel.

"I haven't," I told him. "Not my genre, but I hear it's good."

When he had decided on his next read, he walked to one of the tables near the bar and sat down. "I'll take a drink, if you don't mind. Startin' early today."

"Sure." I mixed his Captain and Coke—a tall single—and sat it in front of him. "How was work?"

"Aw, hell. It's work. That's about all I can say these days."

"Looking forward to retirement?"

He rolled his eyes and then leaned toward me. "They bought me out, ya know. I'm old enough now, they just said why don't I quit in December. Payin' me for a whole nother year. But honest," he began, leaning his head down as if to process his thoughts. "I'll have to find another job. I wouldn't be able to just sit home and do nothin'. I ain't used to not workin'."

I looked at the book Don had laid on the table. *Where the Crawdads Sing*. On first impression, Don was not a person I expected to be an avid reader—at least not one with such diverse taste. Recently, he had branched out from his usual fare, taking suggestions from Niki. He had joined the Boozie Book Club, initially for the free drink and to meet more women. But his insights—even delivered in his lone-star drawl with the occasional colorful expletive—surprised us all.

Another couple stopped in for their late afternoon wine and conversation on the patio. As the store filled up with noise, I let the morning's confrontation slip to the back of my mind. But now I knew David was living perhaps only blocks away. Feeling comfortable with where I was and how the community had accepted me, it was now up to him to make the next move.

Chapter Four

I had rehearsed every conceivable scenario that would bring David and me face to face. In my head, I practiced my responses until I knew them all by heart. Still, that didn't prepare me for the day he walked into the bookstore. We stood apart, both staring, both wondering who would make the first move.

"Becca?" Niki asked as she walked up from her back office.

David's eyes widened. "Becca. Lovely name."

I stayed silent.

"Oh, hi. I didn't realize we had someone in. I'm Niki. Have you been in before?"

"No. First time," he said, never taking his eyes off of me.

As my face reddened under the stare, I turned and walked behind the desk, putting a barrier between us.

"So, welcome to The Nook," Niki said, falling to her role as the consummate business woman. "This is my employee, Becca Mills. Would you like a little tour of the place?"

"Becca Mills," David repeated, still staring in my direction. "Are you married?"

He was baiting me. Taunting me. He knew who had always held the power in our relationship. But he hadn't seen me for five years, nor did he know who I had become. I raised my eyes to meet his gaze. "Yes," I said. "I am." And I smiled at him. "Twenty years now."

It was David's turn to redden. He lost his smile and turned to walk out without saying another word.

Niki stood, aghast. "Wait. What just happened? Did he just hit on you?"

"No," I assured her, fighting to control my body's shake.

"I don't get it." She waited for me to explain something that was inexplicable. When I picked up a book and prepared to enter it into the computer, she said, "You never told me you were married."

"Separated," I said, focusing hard on the task in front of me.

"Well, at four o'clock, we'll have to have a drink, and you're gonna tell me all about it."

She meant well. She always did. But this was a conversation I could not have. I said nothing.

She turned back toward her office. On the way out of the room, she called back, "I think he just hit on you!"

Alone, an uncomfortable silence descended over the room. My hands shook so hard I could no longer work the register. I wanted to follow Niki and ask if I could go home, but I couldn't even stand.

"What have I done?" I asked myself, sickened with regret. "No!" I said aloud, taking a deep breath. "Stop giving him power!"

At the end of my shift, I walked the block to home and spent the night arguing myself out of the anxiety.

David now knew that, not only was I in Baldwin, but that I worked at the bookstore. He could avoid confronting me again, or he could take the opportunity to harass me. I decided that, if it was the latter, I would hold my own and turn his strategy against him.

There was the possibility that our meeting might send him running again. As an adjunct professor, and not a more permanent associate or tenured teacher, his contract would be semester to semester. I started to kick myself for playing my hand too early, but then realized that it relieved some of the pressure to have that moment behind me.

Over the next week, I debated telling Niki the truth. She and I were becoming fast friends, but I didn't want to burden her with something so dark. Trust was also an issue—not that she would intentionally hurt me. It would take exceptional strength for someone of character to resist trying to "help" by letting my secret slip to the authorities, intentional or not. Even the group of regulars at The Nook might overhear something between me and her. I couldn't take the chance.

David did not return. I continued to watch his Instagram, though he seldom posted.

* * *

"It's beautiful," Niki said, staring at the finished watercolor. "You should try to sell your work here at the store."

I shrugged, not sure if The Nook would be the right place to hang that particular piece. "I have other paintings," I said. "Maybe I'll try to get something framed next week."

With no transportation to Lawrence, I had no idea how to get the supplies I needed, but the idea appealed greatly.

"You really should. We can hang them in the lounge area." Her phone rang, taking her away from the conversation.

I glanced out the door to see David and Lena walk past, perhaps on their way to dinner. David had not been in again, but Lena had become a regular—buying off the shelves or ordering a recommendation from a friend. Her and I kept our conversations light, focusing on business. From a number of exchanges, I learned that she was born in Kearney, Nebraska and attended McCook Community College the year after I disappeared. It was a small consolation to know she and David met after I was no longer living in the same house with my husband. I imagined— in his mind—he felt he wasn't cheating. But an unfaithful husband was the least of my worries.

Lena had entered her associate's program with an art specialty. No surprise. By her second year—before getting her certificate—she had moved in with David.

"My parents were so worried," she said, rolling her eyes. "Like, he was so much older and all."

Her dewy-eyed smile betrayed the fact that she felt lucky to have snared him, as if he was such a catch. I would nod and smile, but I kept my responses minimal.

"We want to get married, but he's … ," she had stopped, searching for the right words. "There's a complication."

She never explained what the *complication* was, and I didn't ask. Perhaps David hadn't fully explained it to her. It would be like him to promise Lena something he would never have to deliver. And she was naive enough to think she could convince him otherwise.

I watched them move out of sight before I turned back to the desk where I had laid the watercolor. My recent works showed promise even though I still struggled to free my hand. Niki's suggestion appealed to me on a number of levels. Perhaps I could make extra income. More importantly, after so many years living isolated from the intellectual stimulation that art and culture provided, I craved the interaction. And, admittedly, the accolades.

There was another reason I considered hanging this particular water-color in the store. A darker reason. Assuming David would dare enter the store again, I hoped he might see the work—that it would haunt him as much as it had once haunted me.

When Niki finished her call, she tugged me over to the bar and poured us each a drink.

"Sit," she ordered.

I hesitated, smiling, and then I obeyed. "I know what you're going to ask," I said. "I really can't talk about it."

She studied me for a moment. "Was it that bad?" she finally asked.

"Not until the end."

"Why aren't you divorced?"

"There's a complication," I said, stealing Lena's line.

* * *

"I had a date."

"What did you do?" Madi asked, humoring Don.

"We went to Culvers."

"Culvers? On a first date?" She gave Don an eye roll.

He shrugged. "Well, what can I say? She had a coupon."

Madi continued to wash the bar glasses and place them on the rubber drain pad on the counter behind her. "Hey. Whatever floats your boat."

"Yeah, well. We'll see how it goes."

I sat off to the side and worked on a few random sketches of the bar patrons without their knowing. Don had an angular face with strong chiseled features and a high forehead. He was animated—unable to sit still for any length of time—so it pushed my skills to capture his essence in less than a minute. I realized that I loved the challenge.

At another table, Chris sat silent, staring, contemplating. He often stayed to himself until he had formulated what he wanted to share.

"You know that the Chinese government has figured out how to implant listening devices in books, now." He sat, stone-faced, waiting for anyone to respond. When we kept silent, he continued. "I learned that in my training."

"Sure," Don said, chuckling. "Your CIA training."

Chris squinted at him, holding his gaze. "What? You don't believe me?"

"Well,..." Don began, shrugging his shoulders. "Let's just say, I'm skeptical."

"I'll show you my badge." Chris reached for his phone and pulled up a spinning image of something that looked remotely badge-like. He showed it around, even to me.

"I call bullshit," Jim chimed in, "because there's no name or number on it. A phone image isn't a badge."

Madi caught Jim's attention and asked, "Another one?"

"Sure," he said, taking his wine glass back up to the bar. He leaned over the counter and lowered his voice. "It might help clear the stale air."

Chris didn't appear to be phased by the confrontation. "There's no name and number because I can't give out that information."

"But I thought you said you trusted us," Don reminded him, laughing now. "But maybe you shouldn't."

Don turned his attention back to his friend Kenzie and to the conversation they had been having. "I've had my moments," he said, raising his eyebrows. "When I was sixteen years old, my friends wanted me to help them rob a bank. They wanted me to be the vocal man. To say, 'This is a robbery, and give me all your cash.' I was s'pose to say it in a menacing way."

"Did you do it?" Kenzie asked, grinning at the knowledge that Don had grown beyond his checkered past.

"Well." Don ducked his head and chuckled. "I knew then that I wasn't the bank-robbing kind. I just couldn't do it, man. We had our guns and everything. It was *horrible*. But I knew then, I just couldn't be a thief."

Kenzie looked my direction and winked. Turning back to Don, she said, "You're one bad-ass good guy. You know it?"

When the crowd paired off in conversation, leaving him alone, Chris stood and said his goodbyes. "I'm working security tonight."

No one responded, so he left.

Jim came over to my table. "Can I sit?"

"Sure." I laid my sketchpad in my lap and motioned to the chair across from mine.

"Chris certainly has some issues. I shouldn't have said what I said, but I have no patience for bullshit."

I considered his comment for a moment and then said, "I wonder if he actually has some mental disorder. Perhaps he can't help it."

"Yeah, maybe. I'll try to do better next time." He raised his wine glass in toast. After a sip, he looked over at my sketchbook. "Care to share?"

My instinct was to turn him down, but he seemed legitimately curious. I opened to the page I had just been sketching.

"Ooo, nice! You just did this?"

I nodded. "Working on my one-minute sketches, trying to get back some of the ability I've lost. It's been a long time."

"These look pretty good," he said.

He started to get Don's attention, but I stopped him and flipped the cover back over the drawings. "I'm not ready for anyone else to see these yet. Besides, they're just practice."

"Well," he said with a big grin and a wink, "you practice good."

I was surprised at how strongly I blushed.

Chapter Five

Through the kind assistance of the Open Art members, I managed to get the watercolor of the bowl matted and framed. An off-white mat and a simple black frame, inexpensive. Niki hung it, as promised, in the lounge area on a wall across from the used books.

"How much do you want for it?" she asked. "Just remember that I take twenty percent."

After some calculation, I priced it at three hundred dollars—high enough, I hoped, that it would not sell too quickly. But then, David might never return to the store, so it might have been a moot point.

Lena, on the other hand, continued to frequent the new book section. She gave no indication that David had let slip who I really was. The occasional afternoon, she would stop at the bar and have a *Bookworm* from the list of house cocktails.

"That's such a cute name," she gushed. "So clever, too, that you put a gummy worm in it. And it's a bookstore!" As if we did not know that already.

If Chris happened into the shop while Lena was there, he would spin his heroic tales of intrigue, and she would indulge him, ooing in all the right places. It was painful to see how easily she was taken in. Painful to know that David—a more consummate liar than Chris would ever hope to be—had drawn Lena into his own web of lies. After some consideration, I realized that a life with David may have been all Lena aspired to. She reminded me of my mother. Cloying. Shallow. Hopelessly dependent. She reminded me of who I used to be.

Between The Nook and Open Studio, my social circle continued to expand. My reserved nature did not dissuade those around me from reaching out. More importantly, each of these groups encouraged me in ways I had never experienced. At the bookstore, I became part of Baldwin's literati. At the art center, my reputation as an artist began to grow. I was asked to hang some of my work in the classrooms and in the boutique.

"No more pretty pictures," I said to my mother's wraith. "No more pablum."

Open Art turned into a Thursday afternoon ritual. Though I loved listening in on the conversations and hearing the supportive feedback from the members, I stayed quiet most of the time. It was enough to be immersed in a group of people who seemed to have so much mutual respect for each other.

Soon, a large percentage of my Nook paycheck went for art supplies—drawing pads, pencils, watercolor paper, paints and brushes. I used the table in my apartment more frequently as an art studio than as a dining space. The floor space that, at first, seemed wasted, became a repository for a growing catalog of finished pieces. The best ones I tacked on the walls to study and decide which to frame. I hung three pieces at the arts center, and two more at The Nook. Within a week, one of the new pieces sold.

One evening, I overheard Ajhanae—a Baker student and friend of Madi's—talking about the exhibit in the Holt-Russell gallery at

Parmenter Hall. "It's the new art professor," she was saying. "The work is okay. Not my taste, though."

"I should probably go by and look," Madi said. "Is there a reception? Free food and drink, and all."

Ajhanae laughed. "Probably. And you should know about it for your tours. You can't work in admissions and not know what's going on all over campus."

"True that. Job training *and* free food. Can't beat that."

The following day, I stepped onto the Baker quad now filled with students walking from building to building between classes. Stopping in front of Parmenter, I gathered my courage and then climbed the steps to the hundred and fifty-year-old building. Inside, the entry hall and Lincoln room sat empty as before. I looked right to nod at the security agent, Louis, sitting behind his desk in the small north room. Walking ahead, I pushed through the second set of doors and into the gallery. Inside, I stood for a moment and let my eyes take in first impressions.

Color. Vibrant and curiously cold. My mind flashed back to the jewel-toned walls covered in large abstract canvasses in the McCook house. Some of the works now hanging in the Holt-Russell gallery looked familiar, but it was not that I had seen them before. More that he had been rehashing tired inspiration, drawing on the same processes and tropes he had explored twenty years earlier in his undergrad career.

Fifteen canvasses hung around the walls. Another ten pieces—glass bowls, vases, and abstract sculptures—rested on simple pedestals scattered around the center of the room. I turned to the left and started to inspect each piece.

Halfway through the exhibit, I heard the door to the north wall open. I waited, but he said nothing. I stepped to the next piece, still keeping my back to him.

"Congratulations," I said.

"For what?"

I moved to the next painting. "The job. The exhibit." I leaned in to study the brushstrokes. "Your idyllic life." I imagined his face flushing pink.

"Where have you been?" he asked after a pause.

"Dead," I said, passing two more paintings before turning to face him. "Just not buried."

He held my gaze for a long moment. Finally, he asked, "Why now?"

I stepped up to one of the glass sculptures in the center of the room and resisted the temptation to push it off its stand. "I want to live again. Not the life I had with you. That was never mine."

He moved away from his office door but kept his distance. As I moved slowly around the center of the exhibit, he countered, always staying on the opposite side of the pedestals. It was then that I realized he was afraid of me. Afraid of how I could upset his perfect life. Perhaps he was even physically afraid.

"What do you plan to do?"

That question had haunted me for some time. Before I could answer, a small group of students walked into the gallery. They looked past me and smiled at David. He returned the smile, though it was strained.

"Dr. Sante!" one of them said.

When David didn't correct them, I raised an eyebrow and stared at him. "Good day, *Doctor*," was all I said before leaving the room.

* * *

After the latest confrontation with David, I began to feel the persistent tension in my shoulders ease. I had seen his fear and found it empowering. Laughter had felt like such a foreign language, but it came more easily to me now. I found I could return the easy banter both at The Nook and at Open Art. Don was particularly inspiring with his self-deprecating humor.

"Daaaum," he said the day the bookstore sponsored a chicken salad cook-off. "Did you rig the contest?"

We all agreed that he won fair and square.

"I think ya'll are just being nice."

"Nope," Niki said. "I'm too competitive to let you win."

"That's certainly true," I told him.

Ajhanae took another bite from the center salad. "I voted for presentation," she said. "Yours was the prettiest dish."

Niki complained. "Wait! Were we supposed to pay attention to presentation?"

"It was the hot peppers, then, wasn't it?"

Several of us looked questioningly at Don.

"Daaaum," he said again. "My secret's out." He grinned large and winked at me. "What do I win, anyway?"

"Bragging rights," I said.

"That's it? I thought I'd at least get a trophy or somethun."

Niki stood up and headed behind the bar. "How about a free drink?"

"Hell, yeah!"

Full of chicken salad and side dishes, the bar patrons settled in to watch televised football. I retreated to my corner and enjoyed the game.

I had moved to Baldwin with the idea of getting revenge on David, but as I leaned into my new friendships—and my newfound strength—the desire for retaliation began to fade. For years I thought I had tormented him from the grave only to find that he had moved so completely past my presumed death as if I had never existed at all. That was more painful than the physical blow that sent me into hiding. Now that David had seen me—reincarnated, unshrinking, a threat to his illusion of safety—I wondered if it was worth the emotional energy to push any farther. Perhaps it was enough to shake him out of his complacency and keep him wondering each and every night what the next day would bring. This role reversal—doing nothing more than building a good life right in front of him, in spite of him—might be all the torment I cared to inflict. If I pushed that agenda too far, it could jeopardize the community I was finally building for myself.

At the apartment, I put the losing left-over chicken salad I had made into the fridge and sat down at the table. I thought about what it would take to truly move on. I was not ready to forgive David, but there was a possibility I could forgive myself. Through the myriad of self-help books I had been reading at The Nook, a glimmer of hope appeared. I did not trust myself with a therapist. Not yet. But I realized that one of the greatest methods to affect emotional healing lay at my fingertips.

"Paint what you know," I mumbled. And then I wondered how well I really knew myself.

Chapter Six

Robbie studied the work for several minutes. "It's…," she began, but couldn't find the right word.

"Be honest," I said. "I can take it."

"Powerful is the word that comes to mind." She looked curiously at me. "Where did this come from?"

I hesitated, not sure how much to divulge. "Is it any good?"

"Not good, Becca. It's stunning."

Her comment made me blush, but at the same time, I could feel the pride welling.

"Is this you?" she asked.

I reached for the painting and pulled it up to my chest. "If I tell you, you can't say anything to the others. Promise me."

She nodded.

"This is part of a self-portrait series. I don't know where it will take me, but I feel that I need to confront some things. And I need you not to ask too many questions."

"It's so dark. I can't imagine exposing myself this way." She reached a hand to my arm. "If you ever want to talk, let me know."

Two of the Open Art members pulled up to the curb. I thanked Robbie and shuffled the work to the bottom of the pile I had brought to work on. Before long, the others arrived and took their places around the tables. Noise filled the room as each artist chatted about family or inspiration, or spent time critiquing each other's projects. I always painted safe images in front of them—not quite those pretty pictures my mother had expected of me, but nothing too personal. Robbie was the first person privileged to see inside my head. My heart.

At 4:00, when the session was over, I carried my supplies upstairs to my apartment and then met the group at the local Mexican restaurant down the street. The eight of us sat, as always, at the same two tables— pulled together—and Jordan took our orders.

"The usual?" he would ask as he pointed to each in turn. Most of the group simply nodded, he knew them so well. I still had to spend some time looking over the menu.

After early dinner and margaritas, we said our goodbyes and headed home. Upstairs, I pulled the painting from the bottom of the stack and studied it with a new eye. Robbie had called it powerful. That was all the encouragement I needed to start the next piece.

Time evaporated. At two in the morning, I stepped away from the table and crawled into bed. Even in sleep, my head would not give up the ideas spinning endlessly around and around. In my dreams, I tossed paint in the manner of Jackson Pollock or meticulously drew a hundred straight Agnes Martin lines. I scrambled my own cubist features or softly illustrated my face in the style of the Realists. At one point, I started awake when the face on the canvas began to sag and draw flies from decay.

"*The Persistence of Memory*," I mumbled. The persistence of trauma, I realized.

I had to work The Nook on Friday, but was anxious to get home to the painting. It was all I could think about until it was done. Before I had finished the details, my mind raced to the next concept. The next artwork. It was as if a rift had opened in the fabric of space-time and the whole of my life spilled out onto paper.

There were days when I hated what materialized on the page. My first instinct was to shred those pieces, but I resisted. I had to be totally honest, even with myself, to achieve what I wanted with this project. Even the preliminary sketches had something to say—something that needed to be teased out and laid bare. Of course there would be abandonment issues, thanks to my father's death, but that was not what manifested in the work. Not directly, at least. As the number of finished pieces grew, so did the kernel of a new idea. *What if,* I kept saying over and over.

In early October, my mind had wandered away from my duties at work. One day, I stood staring at the cover of a new-release book. There was nothing much to it—a simple design and a fairly nondescript title. I flipped the cover open and then closed. I repeated the action.

"Becca, could you inventory the cleaning supplies so I know what to pick up at the store tomorrow?"

I flipped the book open and closed again.

"Becca?"

"What?" I asked as I looked over at Niki.

She laughed and asked, "Where's your head today?"

With the book still in my hands, I stared at her, wide-eyed. "I know what I want to do," I said. "I just don't know how to do it."

"How to do what? Inventory?"

I looked at her curiously. "Oh, no. What did you ask?"

She explained again, and I set the book down. Trying to stay on task, I made a list of supplies and added them to her list of liquors to restock. When I had finished, I walked over to Niki's desk and sat down across from her. I hesitated until she had finished typing something.

"I have a project I want to do, but I don't have the tools. I would need help."

"What kind of project?"

"A small construction project. Nothing too complicated. At least, I don't think."

Niki asked the details, but I avoided telling her too much.

"Why don't you ask Don?" she finally said. "I'm sure he'd be happy to help."

I cornered Don the next evening and asked if he would be willing. "I'll buy the supplies and pay you for your time," I said. "Can I just give you the measurements, and you cut and router the pieces? I think I can assemble them."

"Why, hell," Don began in his customary drawl. "I don't need no money for it. Just pay me in alcohol."

"It's not for The Nook," I said, laughing. "This is a personal project. Picture frames."

"Well, you could do better by buying some real frames. They'd be much prettier than anything I could make."

I shook my head. "They won't need to be pretty, just functional. They don't sell what I want in the stores. Can I give you a list of supplies?"

Don agreed, so I sat with him for several minutes and drew out my concept on paper. He worked out dimensions and fine-tuned the construction details.

When we were finished making plans, I gave him a hundred-dollar bill. "This is just to get them started. I'll probably owe you more before they're done."

He hesitated before taking the money. "You sure you don't want to just buy me a case of beer? I'm a pretty cheap hire."

"I'm paying you for your time," I insisted. "No buts."

* * *

Don delivered the frames just before Thanksgiving. I met him on the street outside the apartment and inspected the stack in the bed of his truck.

"I hope you don't mind, but I went ahead and mitered the corners and glued 'em up. I wanted to be sure they were all squared proper."

"Don! You certainly didn't need to do that," I scolded. Secretly, I was glad to be spared work that might have been beyond my skill level.

He picked one up and turned it over for my inspection. "I routered 'em pretty deep, like you wanted. Room enough for glass and backing or whatever else you need to put in there." He glanced at the remaining frames. "That's a mighty lot of pictures you must have."

"A mighty lot," I agreed. I hesitated to invite him, or anyone, into my sanctuary, but there was no way I could carry the frames in one trip. And it was going to be awkward asking Don to wait on the street while I made a number of trips. "Can you help get them upstairs?"

Inside the apartment, Don laid his armload to one side and stood looking around the room. "Daaaaum," he remarked, taking it all in. "Did you do these?"

I nodded, trying not to look too self-important.

"Are these the ones you're gonna frame?"

"Maybe someday," I said. "But I have another project that comes first."

"Mind if I see?" He looked eager to explore the piles I had around the room. When I told him I was not ready to share, he raised his hands and tipped his head. "No problem. I understand."

Before he could excuse himself from the apartment, I slipped two more hundred-dollar bills into his hand.

"Hey, now," he grumbled and started to give one of them back. "You don't owe me near this much."

I refused to except the return. "Your help means that much to me, so please take it."

He stood for another moment, looking as if he wanted to ask something but thinking better of it. I felt guilty after he had gone. Guilty for wanting the space all to myself again.

From one of the kitchen drawers, I retrieved a package of hinges and the screwdriver I had purchased at the local hardware store just two blocks beyond the market. I stacked the frames in the middle of the floor and got to work.

Chapter Seven

Because I would be alone on Thanksgiving Day, several people invited me to dinner with their families—families who knew each other's predilections and peculiarities. As comfortable as I had become with many of my new friendships, it still felt like an intrusion to say yes. I turned them all down, preferring to roast a small chicken for myself and scrutinize the last of the images that needed to be framed. When I had them all in place, I walked around the room, making sure each work measured up.

"I hope it is as good as I think it is," I said aloud. Creating the collection certainly had been cathartic—a personal breakthrough—but that did not mean the pieces would speak to anyone else. Still, I had hope.

The day was warm for late November, and since the campus was closed for break, I decided to take a walk around the quad. The only one about, I spent some extra time around the pond—quiet now because maintenance had turned off the flow of water before it froze. The dragonflies were gone. The tiger lilies at the base of the bridge had shed their petals. I sat for a while beneath the grape arbor and watched squirrels bury what instinct prompted for their survival over the coming winter.

At the north end of the quad, several yards away, I heard the door to Parmenter Hall open and close. Silently, I watched David walk from his office to his car and drive away. He had never been one for family dinners—one of the few things we had in common—but I wondered why Lena was not with him. Perhaps she had gone to visit family on her own. Or maybe she was waiting dutifully at home with the table set for two.

I was surprised at how little his presence affected me. Only months ago, I would have been startled at the sight of him—holding my breath until he had gone, hoping he would not see me encroaching on his space. Now, I simply turned back to the squirrel a few yards away as it clawed a small pit into the earth and dropped in an acorn.

"You'll forget where you put it come January," I said, chuckling at the furry rodent.

The squirrel stood on its hind legs and eyed me for a moment before going back to the business of patting earth over his treasure.

Taking a longer way home, I explored part of the town I had not seen yet. At Fifth and Grove, I stopped to read the signs describing the Old Castle Museum and its history as the first Baker structure and the first college building in the state of Kansas—built a few years before Parmenter Hall. There was something in the history and permanence of the stones that comforted me.

I returned to the apartment just as the sun was going down. Though it was early, still, I let the darkness descend over the room while my eyes adjusted slowly to the faint light from the streetlamps outside. I stared at the images I had created, watched their eyes in the shadows as they appeared to move ever so slightly with my shifting gaze. A sudden shiver sent me groping for the light switch. Blinded, I turned it off again and crawled into bed.

* * *

It snowed lightly the first two days of December and then warmed up again. After our weekly Thursday dinner at the Mexican restaurant, I pulled Robbie aside and asked if she would come up to my apartment. In the hallway, I said, "Please don't judge," and opened the door.

She stepped in and looked around, her eyes wide. "Is this all the furniture you have?"

"Yes, but it's all I need." I tried to sound deliberate.

Her eyes quickly focused on the stacks of drawings and paintings sorted by subject or medium. "You've been busy!"

I walked to the kitchen and retrieved one of the framed pieces. "This is what I wanted to show you," I said, and added, "But only you."

She nodded and then took the piece out of my hands. After inspecting it carefully, she raised her eyes to mine. "I feel privileged," she said, handing it back to me. "It's amazing."

"I have more." I walked back to the kitchen and motioned for her to follow. Along the floor and lower cabinets, I had set the remaining fourteen completed works.

"Seriously?"

I nodded. "It's all I've been doing outside of work and Open Studio. I want to know what you think."

Robbie took her time looking over each one—picking it up carefully and studying it. When she had seen the last one, she turned to me with a look of admiration. "You're very brave," she said. "These are incredible! This should be an exhibit at the gallery."

As much as I loved hearing my work validated, I shook my head. "I'm not that brave." I sat the pieces back into place. "They're so personal, I don't know if I can," I said, holding back the real reason.

"Becca, you have to consider it. I can't imagine these hiding away up here forever."

"I'll think about it," I promised.

After she left, I sat on the bed with my knees folded under me and wondered if, like the art, I could hide up here forever. In Toledo, hiding from the world had been tortuously isolating. In Baldwin, it was a comfort. The change, I realized, had nothing to do with geography.

* * *

Lena came into The Nook to do much of her Christmas shopping. She selected four new books for her parents, some handmade jewelry and soaps, a couple of totes, and a couple of Lauren's handmade bookmarks.

"I'm not sure what to get my two little cousins," she said. "They're only seven and ten."

"We do have a children's book section," I told her, pointing to the north side of the building.

"Great!" She walked to the north room—the first time she had been in that part of the store—and spent several minutes looking at the books and toys.

A few minutes later, I heard her gasp. Curious, I walked around the corner and saw her staring at something on the wall. She looked at me and then back to the painting. Leaning in, she read the signature carefully and then turned to me once more. I could see the recognition in her eyes as her face contorted.

"Becca Mills," she said, glowering at me. "Not Becca Sante?"

I could not answer. I had been so concerned whether or not David would see the painting, I had not even considered Lena. Her eyes turned to ice as she walked past me and left everything she had intended to buy in a pile on the counter.

Feeling guilty and panicked at the same time, I took the painting home that evening. Lena was an innocent, no matter how much I wanted to resent her. Yet, the fact that she had identified the bowl—realized that I was still alive—meant that she could expose me at any moment. It would not matter if she said something to David. He would find some way to talk her down from her hysteria. But if Lena said something to anyone besides David, I could only imagine what punishment I would be due for the laws I had broken.

There was yet another issue I had not considered until now. My reincarnation would simply prove David's claim that I had run away. We were too far past the crime for my side of the story to hold full weight. I could no longer establish any proof of the assault. My scars—healed and barely visible—could have happened at any point in my life. There were no medical records. No police reports. Only my word against David's.

For the second time in my life, I found myself full of dread, watching for some person of authority to walk into my life and ask if anyone had seen "the person in this photo."

* * *

Robbie asked me to her house for Christmas. At first, I declined, but she kept listing the reasons I should accept.

"We're a big Catholic family. The house will be full of people. No one will notice one more."

Odd that her comment should evince the whole of my life. *No one will notice.* I finally agreed, but stumbled when I had to ask for a ride to and from.

"That's no problem," she said. "It's not as if we're miles away."

The day was cold but dry—typical for a Christmas Day in eastern Kansas. Robbie picked me up and drove me the four miles into the country where her house sat on the ridge overlooking the Kaw River valley. From her front porch, the view spanned all the way to Lawrence ten miles away. The air was clean and clear.

I enjoyed watching the younger children through the windows as they spent most of the afternoon outdoors playing ball or walking the woods. Inside, the crowd of adults shared news or reminisced, telling stories that were vastly different from my own childhood memories. I felt happy for Robbie that her family seemed so close-nit, as families should be. But there was an underlying envy for what I had missed as an only child, and for never having children.

After the evening meal, she cornered me and asked if I had considered the exhibit.

"I have to pass," I said, still worried about Lena.

But David's significant other never came back into the store. By mid January, I began to relax again. If she had not let it slip by then, perhaps the storm had passed.

Sales at The Nook slowed. Niki did not require my help as much, so I started volunteering at the arts center. On those days, I would take my sketchpad and pull out whatever was rummaging around in my head. I enjoyed greeting visitors and introducing them to the work in the gallery.

At the end of January, the center hung work from an Iowa artist—a previous resident of Baldwin who had taught art at Baker. She was a print and watercolor artist, working mostly in abstract forms. Listed in Marquis's Who's Who in American Art, she had a stellar reputation in the Midwest. Once the show was hung, I spent several hours studying each piece, comparing her approach to composition and form to what I knew of David's work. And now mine. I should not have. Each person's expression would be unique, yet it was hard not to feel inadequate. Her watercolors were stunning. Her control of the medium, unparalleled. More than the prints, her watercolors fascinated me.

I watched the gallery on most Tuesday afternoons from one to four. Though the numbers were low, they were steady. The majority of the visitors were from Baldwin—loyal repeat viewers. Everyone had interest in the arts, and many were artists themselves. I had large blocks of time to work on my own art, but again, I kept the subject matter light. Visitors would spend time viewing the show in the gallery space, and on their way out, they often stopped at the volunteer desk to comment on what I was doing. Soon, I had made a number of casual new friends with a common bond.

The first Tuesday of February, I sat at the desk inside the courtyard and heard Jeanette in her office.

"No!" she complained to someone on the phone. "We can't lose the show this close to opening. We have nothing to replace it." After a long silence, she spoke again—her voice resigned. "I understand. Maybe Carlo will leave his show up for two months, instead." Another pause. "We'll figure it out."

I went back to my drawing and, as my habit, I tried to tune out the conversation. After another few minutes, Jeanette walked out of the office and stood near me.

"We just lost Kelly's show for the end of March. That's less than two months away." She looked at the drawing on the desk and then eyed me curiously. "Becca. What about you?"

"Oh, no," I said, fiercely shaking my head. "I couldn't."

"Why not?" Her persistent stare turned into a cunning smile. "You'd be perfect," she insisted. "I know you've only been here a few months, but we could use the show to introduce you to Baldwin. Everyone loves your work."

"This is nothing," I told her, looking down at the innocuous sketch.

"Becca! Don't say that. And if it's a matter of getting enough pieces framed, the art center can probably help you with that."

Again, I shook my head. "It's not the frames. I have work ready. It's the publicity."

Her brow furrowed. "What? You don't like your picture taken? I swear," she said, laughing. "Artists are either publicity hogs like Andy Warhol or they are as reclusive as Edvard Munch."

I considered her offer and wondered how I could turn it down. The Lumberyard Arts Center was a small venue in a small town, but having a one-woman show was a first step toward the dream I had had since I was ten. A gallery show meant I could finally call myself an artist.

"Can you promise there won't be any photos of me?"

"Whatever you want," she said, hopping up and down just a little. "You are such a lifesaver!"

That was a moniker I never expected to hear.

Chapter Eight

Twice a week—usually Tuesdays and Thursdays—I would see David walk by The Nook on his way to one of the restaurants for lunch. He was always alone now. Lena had never returned to buy books, and I wondered if she had left David, possibly for good. It was my fault, I reasoned. I scowled at the thought that, in my need for vengeance, I may have unwittingly ended their relationship. But then I realized that Lena was better off moving on.

Most of my attention turned to the upcoming exhibit. Jeanette and the ladies from Open Art spent the month helping me organize my labels and print them out. Robbie was still the only person to have seen any of the collection, so I turned to her for the most assistance. I held Jeanette to her promise of no photos, but she did created a flier using the name of *Becca Mills*, which seemed safe enough. And the title: *Behind the Mask*. We planned the refreshments and wine for opening night—something I had been accustomed to as a professor's wife—and I braced myself for my first real moment in the limelight.

The third Friday in March came, and I snuck into the art center before six. I paced the courtyard, wringing my hands, and trying to silence my mother's voice. "You're wasting paper," she had said as she tossed her least favorite of my ten-year-old paintings into the fireplace. "And what is this?" She held it up. An abstract. "I'm not buying you any more paint if this is what you do with it." Silently, helplessly, I had watched the flames curl the edges of each page and then crawl across the surfaces. The yellow fire ate all of the vibrant reds, the brilliant blues, the greens and purples, until it, too, died to black.

I closed my eyes and shuddered.

Jeanette came in to help set up the food table. "You look beautiful," she said, noticing the second-hand designer shift I had purchased from a local thrift store.

Not comfortable with makeup, I steered clear of liner and lipstick, but did add a hint of mascara—just enough to define my eyes. I had pulled my shoulder-length hair into a French twist and secured it with a tortoiseshell clip, letting the ends flair in whatever direction they chose. Artsy, but not flamboyant.

"The show is magnificent," she said. "Are you ready?"

"I'm terrified," I told her.

She linked one elbow in mine. "Just let the work speak for itself."

I moved to a corner of the courtyard and sat on one of the benches. My stomach churned mercilessly as I waited for the first patrons to arrive. Robbie, thankfully, came early enough to offer support.

"You look nervous," she said. She went to the wine table and reached for a glass, pouring it full. "Here, drink up." When I had polished it off, she poured another and said, "Now, this is the one you carry around to sip on."

"Thanks." I let the alcohol do its job, cutting my nerves a bit.

Just before 6:30, Sandy and Sharron arrived. They stopped by the table to say their hellos and pick up wine and hors d'oeuvres. Sandy grabbed me by the arm and pulled me into the gallery. "I want to get a personal tour," she said.

"Me, too," Sharron said, following us into the room. "You've kept this such a secret."

I stood, awkwardly, as they stepped up to the first piece titled "Roots." Sandy looked at the graphite drawing behind the glass—me, highly detailed, as a young teen with only a faint smile on my lips. After a moment, she turned to me with questioning eyes and then turned back to inspect the frame. It was two frames, actually, hinged on the left. On the right, a small knob invited the viewer to open it like a book.

"Can I?"

I nodded and held my breath.

The door swung open, and Sandy caught her breath. The second image, initially hidden by the first, was a technicolor painting of me at the same age but frozen in a silent scream. Layers of my mother's scowling image smothered my young face. The edges of the paper had been burned—carefully, strategically—with a match.

"Wow," was all she could say. She exchanged glances with Robbie who I had not realized was standing behind me.

"Amazing, isn't it," Robbie said.

Sharron echoed her comment. "Amazing. And powerful."

"That's exactly what I told her."

I let them continue around the room as I held back. There seemed to be no need for me to explain any of the work. But I watched and listened as they studied the first twelve—various stages of my life, various public masks. Various hidden traumas.

When they came to the thirteenth piece, I shuddered. The mask—the drawing they initially saw—looked exactly as I did today. Middle-aged. Austere. But with shorter hair. When they opened the door, the painting behind was of my upper body—eyes closed, pale, shrouded in leaves—with a gash on my forehead and blood running down my face. Sandy looked once more at the title of the piece. "Death Mask."

She turned to find me across the room, her eyes questioning what the painting meant. I simply shrugged.

Work number fourteen was titled "Zoe." The masked image showed a women with a generous smile and kind eyes, captured at the peak of her health. She held a book in her hand. When Sandy pulled open the door, she saw a woman bedridden, shriveled and bald. Tubes and wires—mimicking the shape of wings—ran from the woman's body to a number of machines monitoring corporeal functions. The words "See you soon" had been layered over the foot of the hospital bed. If the three women had looked to me for answers, I had turned away.

The final piece, number fifteen, was titled "Wings." The cover mask was an image of David, recognizable to those who might know him. His body was staked to the ground, his chest and stomach flayed open to the twenty vultures—one for each year of our marriage—hovering around the edges of the drawing. Behind this mask, in technicolor, I stood with my arms wide, my face raised, my body hovering effortlessly above David's chest as if I had just been freed. Behind my arms, the wings of a Phoenix flamed into the sky.

I would never have imagined the response. As the crowds filed in, I retreated to my corner and shook my head any time Jeanette looked my way, questioning. She kept her promise, steering anyone away who wanted to talk to me. Robbie sat with me most of the night. As the show was winding down, Jeanette informed me that seven pieces had sold, to be delivered after the show was over. I let out the breath I had been holding most of the night.

Just before the art center closed, a lone man stepped into the courtyard and walked directly into the gallery. From my corner, I could not see him again until he was halfway through the exhibit. He wandered along the walls, opening doors, spending time concentrating on each work. I held back, studying his responses. When he stepped in front of "Wings," I had a clear view of him as his eyes darkened, his face reddened. Then he opened the door.

By his reaction, I knew the piece was worthy. No matter what he said now, I had my validation.

When he stepped out of the gallery, he searched the courtyard until he found me. Alone. He walked over and stood looking down where I sat. I wondered if he would try to cut me with his words or demean the work, but he said, "It's good."

"It's honest."

His eyes narrowed. "Now what?"

I studied the lines on either side of his mouth and around his eyes. "Did you even cry for me?"

His body jerked slightly as if he had just been pricked with some sharp object.

"I don't hate you, David. Not anymore."

"But you want to screw up my life."

"I did, once," I admitted. "I'm sorry about Lena."

His expression soured.

"Will she ever forgive you? Or me?"

In the past, he had always been the one so sure of himself, but now he looked lost. This was a difficult expression for me to process. He stepped back and glanced through the door at the exhibit one more time. Without another word, he left.

* * *

Niki insisted on celebrating at The Nook. The usual crowd of misfits gathered around to congratulate my success.

Jim bought me a shot of double-chocolate vodka even though I was now due several hundred dollars from the arts center. "Congrats," he said.

Don raised his glass. "Here's to art! Don't know why, but let's drink anyways."

I raised my glass and cried, "Salud!"

"Sa-what?" Don asked.

"It means *to your health*," Jim explained.

"Heeell," Don said. "If that's the case, I'm livin' to a hundred." He laughed and began a story about his friends George and Big Walter, two of the hardiest men he had ever known.

"George had been complaining about a toothache all night, and we were gettin' tired of hearing it. Big Walter said, 'I can pull it!' I admit, we were pretty drunk. Well, Big Walter goes out to his truck and gets a pair of pliers. We're standing there thinking George is gonna back out but, daaaum if he didn't open his mouth. Big Walter, he just grabbed the tooth with that pair of pliers, his knee on George's chest, and worked that tooth right out. And we all looked at it. Hell, there wasn't nothin' wrong with it! George is like, it's the wrong tooth! Everybody in that place started laughing." Don dipped his head and smiled. "Except George, of course."

I cringed, but couldn't help laughing along with the rest.

"Big Walter, he was a hard ass. I remember one night we got in a fight over somethun, I don't remember what. I was poundin' on him, and all I did was hurt my hands hittin' him in the head. Daaaum!"

I considered Don's life, his wide-open approach to everything he did, and I was envious.

Jim raised his glass of wine to distract me. "Congratulations, again," he said. "It was an interesting art show."

"Just interesting? Not pretty enough for you?"

"I didn't say that. It just takes a bit to process, is all." He lost his smile for a moment. "How much of that was real?"

"Too much," I said.

"And the death mask?"

All I could do was raise my glass for another toast.

Chapter Nine

David's second semester at Baker was coming to a close. He continued to avoid the bookstore, but many of his students came in on the nights Madi worked. I heard them regurgitating the latest gossip about who liked the new adjunct and who might openly flirt with him.

"Carry said she'd sleep with him if he wasn't married," Ajhanae told her friends as they sat at the bar. "She thinks he's sexy. I just think he's old."

"He isn't married," Madi said from behind the counter. "He had a significant other, but they're not married."

"How do you know?"

Madi pulled a glass from the sanitizer in the sink and leaned forward. "Because I work in Admissions, and I know all of the teachers. Besides, she left him."

The three girls at the bar eyed each other. "SOMEBODY TELL CARRY!" they joined in chorus, laughing.

"Yeah, well," Madi said, dunking another glass. "I agree with Ajhanae. He's old."

I smiled from the corner of my table. I suppose that meant I was old, too—at least in their eyes—but I realized that I had never felt so young. Not even in my teens. I was surprised to hear my own voice break into the conversation.

"Do you think they will pick him up for next year? Isn't he just an adjunct?"

Madi looked at me, surprised by the question. "Maybe. I mean, I don't think they have anyone to replace him."

Ajhanae turned to me. "He's an okay teacher. Maybe they'll make him associate soon."

"Or a full professor."

"They can't do full professor yet," I explained. "He never finished his doctorate." My cheeks grew warm as soon as I said it.

"Are you sure?" Ajhanae asked. "Everyone calls him Dr. Sante."

"Just the students," Madi said, countering. "I don't think I've ever heard another teacher call him that."

I tried to sink back out of sight, but now the girls were looking to me for an answer. "I read his intro on the Baker website," I said. "I'm sure it read *ABD*. Isn't that 'All but dissertation?'"

Madi brought up a wet hand dripping with suds and pointed at me. "True that," she said, and the girls turned back to her. But before I could completely disconnect from the conversation, Madi added, "Becca, maybe you should date him. You're both artists."

Before I could stop myself, I started laughing—far too long and far too loud.

The rumors began in mid-June. I had been in Baldwin over a year, and The Nook had become not just a workplace, but my regular haunt on my days off. Madi and Lauren both lived in town, and without summer classes, their hours at the store picked up. I continued to eavesdrop on the campus gossip.

"Madi!" Lauren called from the front desk. "Did you hear? The police questioned Dr. Sante yesterday." She stepped around the desk and walked over to the bar area.

"I think we determined he's not a doctor," Madi corrected as she stocked the beer cooler.

Lauren pursed her lips. "Well, no matter. They showed up at his house yesterday. My neighbor said they walked all around the yard looking for something."

My heart skipped a beat. I sat quietly in the overstuffed chair near the front door and pretended to read the book in my hands.

"That is weird," Madi agreed. "Ajhanae said someone came by Administration a couple of weeks ago with questions about his girlfriend. Wasn't she the one who always bought the romance novels?"

"Oh, yeah," Lauren said. She turned to me. "You remember her, don't you Becca?"

I looked up and nodded, then quietly turned back to my book.

"Lena, I think. You know, I never saw her second semester."

"That's because she left him," Madi reminded her. "Or maybe she didn't like Kansas."

Lauren grinned at her. "Maybe she didn't like Mr. Sante anymore."

The words in front of me blurred, and a tear dropped onto the page. I wiped it away quickly and shut the book. "Surely not," I said to myself as I replaced the book on the shelf and walked out. Halfway down the street, I stopped and looked back at the corner of campus. He would not try it twice. Not after realizing that the first time had failed.

"Lena," I blurted before turning around to head home. I stopped at the corner of Eighth and High to decide which way to go. I wanted to turn right. To climb the steps. Hide. But concern got the better of me, and I turned left toward the library. Perhaps I would not find anything, but I had to know.

I logged on to my Instagram and started combing through David's posts. He had never been one to tout his relationship with Lena online. In fact, most who did not know him would think he was unattached—the playboy artist. There were hundreds of photos of him surrounded by young girls at various parties and nightclubs. Some of the older photos included Lena and some did not. After scrolling back through the months, I switched to Google and typed in "Lena Love." Pages and pages of suggestions popped up. Most were dating sites with the name *Lena* buried somewhere in the copy or user lists.

Leaning back in my chair, I thought of all the ways I could narrow the search. She had told me, once, where she was from. I finally typed in "Lena Love Kearney Nebraska Missing." And there it was. An article from three months earlier. The family claimed that their daughter must have succumbed to some tragic circumstance, that she would never just disappear without a word. The article was vague about the details, but neighbors had implied some estrangement between the young woman and her parents. The possible truth resonated when I realized that the family had not reported her missing until late March though I had not seen her since December.

"The older man," I thought. That was what she had said. Her parents did not like the age difference between her and David. It was a good enough reason for some family members to lose contact with each other. David certainly knew how to pick partners with few ties, and he could expertly drive a wedge between them if the ties were tenuous enough. I doubted it was a conscious act. But his need to be the alpha in any relationship meant he sought out those who fawned over him and played a subordinate role. Twenty years ago, I had been his Lena.

Something else worried me. The timing of her parents police report coincided with the opening of my exhibit. I could not imagine any connection, but the coincidence seemed bizarre. I printed off a copy of the article and took it home.

***

Niki sat at the chess table near the window and stared at the board. Creighton, a local lawyer, watched her eyes as she tried to undo the damage she had already done to her collection of pieces. She was a fierce competitor, and each loss merely strengthened her resolve to win.

"Dammit," she said, finally giving up. "Okay. I know it's checkmate. You win."

Creighton bowed his head respectfully. "It was a good game," he said.

"Someday I'm gonna figure this out and kick your butt," she told him.

"Anybody else?" he asked, looking around the room.

Ajhanae stepped off of her bar stool and volunteered. Creighton explained the movement of the pieces, and they spent the next thirty minutes playing a one-sided game.

I sipped my vodka and swayed subtly to Ajhanae's playlist coming from The Nook TV. It was good to decompress in the company of people who did not know my past or the complications of my present.

Madi worked the bar. Niki split her time between her publishing company or the bookstore and relaxing with the regular patrons. I sat in my usual corner and hoped that no one would notice me. But, of course, someone did.

Jim walked in and said his hellos to everyone. Before I could stop him, he had sprung for my second vodka.

"Cheers," he said, raising his glass but not drinking as custom required.

I took a sip of my drink and sat the rest on the table away from me.

"What's up?" he asked. "You look," he began, and then lowered his chin and said, "a bit introspective, perhaps?"

"Not much. You look chipper," I said, trying to divert the conversation.

He watched me for a few moments and then sat his drink on the table. "Seriously," he said. "What's up?"

I took in a long breath. "Can we go upstairs?" I asked.

He raised his eyebrows. "Your place?"

"I just need some time outside of myself. Does that make sense?"

He studied me for a few moments and then nodded. We left the store and walked the block to my apartment. Inside, I motioned for him to sit in the chair while I sat back on the bed and propped my pillow against the wall behind me.

"Nice place you have here," he said, grinning and winking. "You have about as much furniture as I do."

I started to give him the same line I gave Robbie when she first saw the room. Instead, I chose to be direct. "When I moved in, I didn't think I would be staying this long. I didn't think there would be a reason to."

"And now you have a reason?"

"Several," I said, nodding. "I love Baldwin. I don't want to move again."

"Why would you?"

I leaned my head against the wall and closed my eyes, but still the tears began to fall down my cheeks.

Jim stood up and walked to the bed. He held out his arms and said, "May I?"

I slid off the bed and let him wrap me in a tight hug. We stood that way for several seconds until his arms loosened, and I stepped back.

Embarrassed, I said, "I invited you here for another reason."

He nodded. "I thought you might have. But now is not the time."

"You understand?"

He took my elbow and guided me back onto the bed, and then he returned to the chair. "I would never take advantage," he promised. "Not that I'm not interested."

"Thank you for the understanding. And for the flattery."

"Well, let's just say that, if the time is ever right, you let me know. But it's your call."

My eyes widened. "My word. You're a feminist."

"Through and through," he said. "I get that from my daughters."

I shook my head. "I think your daughters get it from you."

We talked for a while longer before Jim grew interested in the stacks of art. I let him look through most of them, only stopping him when he reached for the preliminary sketches for the Mask pieces—some even darker than what ended up on the walls of the gallery.

When he came across a drawing entitled "Hettie," he spent a few extra minutes looking at it. "Wow. Those eyes."

"Would you like it?"

He turned to me, questioning. "How about I buy it from you."

"No, you won't. It's either take it for nothing or it stays here."

At first, I thought he was going to put it back, that I would have to pressure him more, but he finally held it up and smiled. "It will have a special place on my wall."

"Good."

I escorted him to the door, and he held out his arms for one more hug.

"And thanks again for letting me change my mind."

He kissed me on the cheek.

After he left, I sat back on the bed and thought about Lena.

Chapter Ten

The university classes ramped up again, and it appeared that David had been contracted for another year. I continued to search out information on Lena's whereabouts, but there was little to be had. Her family tried to keep the story in the spotlight, but when the news outlets moved on, her father took his case to social media. There, unfortunately, the story became bait for a number of crazies—a never-ending loop of misinformation and conspiracies. I thought of my mother.

I hated to admit that this was the first time I had considered her suffering. Too caught up in my own, and perhaps seeking retribution for the slights of my childhood, I buried any sense of compassion I might have felt for her.

I wondered how hard she had tried to find me—throwing the story of her loss out to the world, begging for attention from a hundred media outlets. It certainly brought her another level of martyrdom she could milk in front of her friends.

As soon as I had that thought, my cheeks caught fire, burning with guilt.

"You've become what you hated most in her," I grumbled. Bitter. Selfish. I thought of the unflattering way I'd portrayed her in the images behind my vapid masks, of her words scolding me for daring to expose the underbelly of our relationship. Her circle of friends—as astringent and reproachful as she—would have thought it a scandal.

My life was quite scandalous, actually. Full of secrets. My thoughts circled back to Lena—the innocent in all of this.

"Please let her be alive."

I took my concerns to The Nook and spent most of the day working quietly and alone. Chris showed up early in the afternoon, but I didn't have tolerance for his delusions. I let Niki entertain him at the bar while I hid behind the front desk and considered what my next move should be.

In Baldwin, I had certainly done the damage I'd intended—just to the wrong person. David still appeared to be unscathed. Was that because I had not acted directly against him? I had not, yet I couldn't decide if it was a lack of courage or a diminishing lack of desire. I had played this charade for over six years. It was time to make my move or forfeit the game.

Jim interrupted my thoughts as he wandered in for his weekly drink. When I finished my work and checked out for the day, I went to sit with him in the bar.

"I'm buying my own drink tonight," I insisted and had Niki pour my usual vodka.

Once I sat down, he said, "You never answered my question."

"Which one was that?"

"Why you might need to move again." He watched my smile disappear. "It's okay. If it's too personal, no need to answer."

I sat contemplating my glass until I could sense his discomfort. Before he could speak again, I asked, "Have you ever done something you regretted? Truly regretted, down to your bones?"

"We all have, haven't we?"

"No, I'm not talking about divorces or cheating on a spouse or spanking a child in a moment of weakness." I couldn't imagine Jim doing anything more dastardly than what I'd already mentioned.

His eyebrows lifted.

"I'm talking about something so profound that it impacts someone else's ability to live their life. Something you can't smooth over or take back."

"Sounds like murder," he said, chuckling. He sobered when he saw the look on my face. "That drawing of the man with his chest flayed open. That wasn't your ex, was it?"

"No. He's not my ex." I hoped the white lie was not obvious. "And he's not dead."

"That's a relief," he said, raising his glass. "I really couldn't imagine you with an ax in your hand."

I winced, remembering another trauma in a small hotel in Iowa. Sensing that my barriers had gone up again, Jim let me change the subject. Though our friendship had grown strong, I couldn't chance sharing things that might color his opinion of me. Then again, maybe the mystery was part of the attraction.

* * *

Niki took off work on Wednesdays. With Lauren back in school, it was my duty to open the shop. As soon as the sign lit up, a young woman got out of her car and stepped in. She waited at the entrance, her eyes searching the first two rooms. When she saw me, she deliberately stepped in my direction.

"Can I help you?" I asked.

She stood quietly, staring, like she was taking the measure of me.

My eyes widened. Her hair was darker and shorter, but I knew that face—the face I once looked on with disdain. I couldn't stop myself from running up to her, throwing my arms around her, hugging her in great relief. "Lena!"

She let me hug her, but she did not return the gesture. I pulled back a bit and grabbed her shoulders to look more closely at her face. She was scowling, so I backed up a few steps. Of course, she would still hate me.

"You must be Rebecca," she said.

The look on my face brought a smile to hers, but only briefly.

"I'm Gena. Lena's sister."

My mouth dropped open. "Twins?"

"Not twins." She moved farther into the store and looked at the bookshelves. "We're eighteen months apart," she said, turning to face me again. "What do you know about my sister?"

For a moment, I could not speak. I had difficulty taming my thoughts. I remembered Lena's words to me—that I had a twin out there somewhere—and wondered if she was playing some retaliatory game with my head.

Angry now, she raised her voice and repeated, "What do you know about my sister?"

"Nothing," I finally said. "I … we … she was here in December, and I haven't seen her since." I scrambled to think up some benign explanation of our last meeting, the day Lena saw the painting.

"I know who you are," she said, accusing. "Why are you here?"

"I work here."

Gena shook her head. "Why are you in Baldwin?"

My body began to shake. I backed up to one of the reading chairs and sat down. When I could speak again, my voice was weak. "Have you seen David? Does he know you're here?"

"Why?" she asked. "Are you two playing some kind of game?"

"No game," I promised and looked up at her. "At least not in the way you think."

"What is that supposed to mean?" She reached into her purse and pulled up her phone. "I should call the police right now."

"NO!" I jumped from the chair and ran to her. "Please, no police."

When I reached for her hand, she jerked the phone away and started to press the nine.

"Stop!" I screamed. "There's so much you don't know. So much I need to explain first."

Her finger stayed poised over the numbers, but she hesitated. Watching me closely, she saw my expression change from panic to sorrow. I raised my hands and backed away.

"Explain."

I had no choice but to trust her. "Lena may be a victim, but so was I."

"That doesn't make sense," she said. "You're here. You're alive. And David knows you're alive."

"He does now," I said, faintly. I caught movement through the window and realized a customer was about to walk in on us. "Gena, before you go to the police or have any contact with David, I need to tell you everything I know. But I can't do it here."

Deb walked in with her watering can and turned to me. "Hey there! Come to give the plants on the patio another round before the frost next week." She headed to the sink at the bar.

I turned back to Gena and lowered my voice. "I get off at four. Meet me here," I pleaded.

She hesitated and then nodded before walking out.

* * *

Madi was on shift, and I waited near the door for Gena to arrive. Ten minutes after four, she started up the steps. I moved outside and suggested we sit at one of the patio tables. No one else was around, so I chose the table farthest from the street.

"Lena was a regular," I began, keeping my voice low. "She came in every week after the semester started."

"That doesn't explain why you're here."

"I know. I will. Just let me tell you what I know about Lena first." She nodded, so I continued. "In early December, she noticed a painting on the wall of the store. A painting I had done of one of David's art pieces. She recognized it and then me. She left before I could explain.

"I was terrified she would go to the authorities, just like I'm terrified that you will."

Gena straightened in her chair. "So you killed her."

"No! Oh my god, no! I never saw her again."

A couple, out for a stroll with their dogs, walked past us. I stayed quiet until they were out of hearing range.

I lowered my head. "When I didn't see her at the start of spring semester, I first assumed she wasn't coming back in because of me. Then I heard the students say she'd left David. I was relieved."

"She did leave him," Gena confirmed. "She moved home at Christmas."

My eyes lit up. "So she is alive," I blurted. "Somewhere."

Still cautious, Gena said, "When Lena came home, she was devastated. She and David had had a huge fight. She couldn't believe the coincidence that you were in Baldwin, or that David didn't tell her."

"It was my fault," I said, closing my eyes. "But I honestly thought it was for the best."

"She told me about you. That you really had run off just like David had said all those years. But then she couldn't understand why he wouldn't turn you in when you were here, living in the same town. Unless he already knew."

"David has his own secrets," I said before a moment of panic rose in my chest. I looked directly at her. "Who did you tell?"

She studied my fear, and I realized that she took it as genuine. "No one. Lena made me promise."

I let out a long breath. "Gena, I need to hold you to another promise. You cannot let David know you're in town. It's imperative."

"Why?" she asked, watching me. "What are you afraid of?"

"I'm not certain yet, but there's more you need to know."

It took some convincing, but Gena finally agreed to come up to my apartment even though she seemed skittish of the idea. Once inside, I closed the door but made a point of showing her it was unlocked.

"I'm not the one who would hurt you," I said.

She stood near the door while I walked to the edge of the bed and sat down. I motioned to the chair, but she didn't move.

I began with the night David and I fought, and he struck me. I told her everything that happened—his crime, the cover up, and my escape.

"He buried you alive?" she questioned in horror.

"He thought I was dead."

"That he'd murdered you!" she corrected. At that point, she walked across the room and sat down hard in the chair. She clenched her hands and started yelling at the ceiling, "He murdered my sister!" Pounding her fists on her knees, she continued to cry out.

I walked over and knelt in front of her, trying to calm her. "Maybe," I said, not wanting to give false hope. "But we don't know anything at this point."

Sobbing now, she grabbed my hands. "You can testify against him. Becca, you have to!"

I pulled her from the chair and walked her to the edge of the bed. We sat together for a long time as I held her, listened to her heartbreak.

"I never intended to hurt Lena," I said when she'd quieted. "I wish I'd had her courage. The courage to walk out on David."

Gena pushed away and shook her head. "She'd gotten over her anger. After all, she didn't believe he had really done that much wrong? Just kept your secret." She stared out the window for a long moment before turning back to me. "Lena had no idea what you suffered. So she decided to come back to Baldwin and try to work it out between them."

My smile was cunning. "David has always been persuasive. And he certainly knows how to pick a naive partner."

I saw Gena flinch.

"I'm sorry. That was cruel."

"Perhaps," she agreed, "but it's also true."

"When was the last time you talked to her?"

"She left Kearney the first of March. She called me from Hays where she was spending the night. No one has seen or heard from her since." She clenched her fists again.

The sun had set, and the apartment was going dark. I stood to turn on a light.

"Becca."

When I turned to face her, there was fire in her eyes.

"You have to testify," she said again.

I shook my head. "If I came forward now, it would do more to exonerate him than it would to imply his guilt. He's right. I was a coward. I simply ran away."

"But he assaulted you! He tried to cover up a crime."

"Yes, but where's the proof? The only evidence is this." I lifted the hair away from my forehead to show the scar. "It's healed. It could have happened two years ago. Or ten."

For a moment, she looked defeated, and then her anger flared again. "He can't get away with this," she seethed.

"No," I said, sitting beside her again. "No, he can't."

CHAPTER ELEVEN

October in Baldwin was a busy affair. For over fifty years, the third full weekend was reserved for a grand celebration of hand-made arts and crafts, food, music, and a parade. The Maple Leaf Festival drew visitors from two states—most from the greater Kansas City area. For two days, the town swelled from four thousand locals to over thirty-thousand out-of-town pedestrians eager for smoked turkey legs, funnel cakes, and kettle popcorn. Booths lined High Street from Sixth to Eighth, and Eighth Street from Chapel to Indiana. Visitors could choose from soaps and bath balms, photography and oils, purses and printed tees, jams and soups mixes. The selection seemed limitless.

In the middle of High Street, outside my apartment window, a carnival sat up late Thursday night. Until midnight, I lay in bed and listened to the clang of metal on metal as the various rides were hammered into place and their spidery arms rose up from the pavement. The festivities ran from late Friday evening until late Sunday—flooding my apartment with flashing lights, a drone of voices, and music that sounded as if it came from a calliope.

I had been in Baldwin for the previous festival, but hid out then, not yet wanting to run into David. This year, I took full advantage, casually wandering the street, inspecting goods I knew I would not buy, tasting the fatty and sugary delicacies I avoided the rest of the year. I found more anonymity in the crowd than there had been in the empty streets, but still I kept a wary eye. David had never been one for community activities though I could imagine Lena dragging him everywhere and insisting he appreciate whatever trinket she fawned over. But this year, I assumed he would be alone, and therefore avoiding the crowds.

Inside the Lumberyard Art Center, various artists had rented small booth spaces to sell their wares. Thursday afternoon's Open Art group pooled their resources and rented a double space to hang twenty pieces. I agreed to man the booth for three hours on Saturday afternoon, using the time to quick-sketch faces from the crowd. The activity attracted a few curiosity seekers to stare over my shoulder. Unless they spoke to me, I kept my head down and continued to work.

"You're drawing skills have improved a great deal," a man's voice said.

I took in a sharp breath and then forced my shoulders to relax.

"Working on your next exhibit?"

I rested the graphite stick on the side of the sketchpad and raised my head. "Just enjoying the festival," I said. "I'm surprised to see you out and about."

He stepped into the booth and ran his eyes around the display. "Some of these are not bad."

"For a bunch of amateurs," I said, finishing his thought for him. He didn't deny it. I bristled at his attitude—one I had been the recipient of many times.

He made a cursory glance at the paintings and started to walk away from me.

"I hear Lena is missing," I said, watching his back go rigid. He hesitated only a moment and then walked out of the art center.

If I had been expendable—no use to him—I might have been more cautious. As it stood, I was the one person on this earth he could not harm. Not now. Not while he was under suspicion for a second disappearance. It emboldened me. Made me reckless.

I finished my shift at the art center and walked home.

* * *

The Nook had done an incredible amount of business over the festival weekend. Niki not only sold three times her weekly tally in books and merchandise, but the bar quintupled its business. Madi made a killing in tips, and Lauren made her biggest commission ever on the stickers and custom bookmarks she sold through the store.

Niki placed a number of orders over the next few days to restock the shelves before the Christmas shopping season began. Every three or four days, boxes arrived from book distributors, game manufacturers, gift merchandisers. She gave me extra hours, and I stashed some of the extra pay to invest in my next round of art supplies—large heavy-weight drawing paper and a full set of graphite pencils from hard to soft. I had my inspiration.

I tried to drop a subtle hint at Open Art one Thursday. "Where is the best place to get quality drawing papers?"

"There's a craft store in Lawrence," Roma suggested.

"Maybe, but I was thinking something bigger and heavier weight than they carry. Maybe Arches hot press single sheets, twenty-two by thirty. Is there a place in Lawrence I can get that?"

Susan shook her head. "Probably the closest place would be in Overland Park."

I was landlocked in Baldwin. I had too much pride to ask outright, so I simply dropped my shoulders and sat quietly at my table.

Robbie noticed. "I'm going to the city next week. You wanna ride along?"

If it had been anyone else, I would have said no. But Robbie and I had become close since my exhibit, so I felt it would be less of an imposition.

"Only if I can pay for the gas," I said.

She started to resist, but I told her I wouldn't go any other way.

The next week, we drove to Coldsnow's, and I made my purchases. Afterward, Robbie asked if I wanted to stop for lunch. We found a bistro nearby and sat down.

"Let me buy you lunch," I said.

"Not if you're also paying for gas. Besides, I was coming up anyway."

I smiled at her. "Somehow, I think that's not the complete truth. And I appreciate your offer to drive."

We ordered and then relaxed with our drinks until the food came.

"Becca," she began and then hesitated. "I can only imagine what your life has been, especially after seeing the exhibit. I just want you to know …"

"Thank you," I said, stopping her. "When the time is right, I'll tell you everything."

Our food came, so we spent a few minutes tasting and commenting on the cuisine. When we were halfway through the meal, I put my fork to the side and looked up.

"I have a new concept in mind."

Her eyes lit up. "Care to share?"

I shook my head. "Not yet, but I don't think the general public will find it quite as ... sensational as the last show."

We ate a little longer before she said, "It doesn't need to be. You don't have to prove yourself again."

"Isn't that what artists strive for?"

No one would understand the purpose of my series, and I couldn't tell Robbie why proving myself no longer mattered. This next project was not for me. It was for Lena.

* * *

The first weeks in November, I started checking at the post office for a general delivery package for Becca Mills. When it arrived, I hurried the envelope home and opened it quickly. Several eight-by-ten glossies slid out.

I studied them for days before choosing which one to tackle first. After a number of preliminary sketches trying to develop the concept, I pulled out one of the larger costly drawing sheets and put my first graphite line to paper. I worked late into the night, past my curfew, finally giving in to the idea that I had to open the shop the next day.

Each week, I labored for hours to produce one larger-than-life work. Using a number nine hard graphite pencil, I strategically carved faint grooves into the page before shading over them with a soft number six. The effect produced extremely fine detail that made the photo-realistic drawings come alive. I thought how fitting it was that I'd learned the technique from David.

The late nights continued through November and December. I worked diligently, secretly, on each piece, not sure when—or if—they would be displayed. The series was intended for only one set of eyes, but I had no clear idea how to guarantee he would see it.

Just before semester's end, I was working and caught David out of the corner of my eye. I watched out the window as he walked across the street. He started to pass by The Nook, glancing briefly at the building, but stopped. He stared at the large leaded-glass window in the original part of the house that looked in on the children's section. For a moment, he squinted, and then his body jerked as if he'd been gut punched. Rather than continuing on to downtown, he turned and walked back toward campus. I smiled and went back to work.

Chapter Twelve

"You know, some of the best mad scientists solved their equations while eating pizza," Don was saying.

Chris stared thoughtfully into space for a moment—his habit before speaking. "That's not true," he finally said, his voice authoritative.

Don frowned and eyed him suspiciously. "Now, how would you know what the hell was true and not true?" Then he mumbled under his breath, "Mr. CIA."

If Chris took offense, he did not let on. "Well, I'm just saying, how would you know? You weren't there."

"Heeelll," Don barked at him. "It's just a damn joke. I mean, c'mon."

Jim and I sat at a corner table and tried to ignore everyone around us. The bar was busy enough that we could huddle into our own conversation and talk in our normal voices without being overheard. He asked me how life was in general and what I was working on. I kept my responses vague.

"Still finding it hard to trust, eh?"

I lowered my eyes. "You've noticed."

He twirled his wine glass a couple of turns while studying my face. "If half of what you shared in your exhibit is close to the truth, I can't say I blame you."

"Paint what you know," I quipped, and forced a tight smile.

He didn't pursue that thought any further.

Niki's husband, Jeff, arrived with the weekly liquor order. He looked at me as he walked by with a case. "We have your chocolate vodka," he assured me and grinned.

I gave him a thumbs up. Don and Jim helped him carry in the rest of the order while Niki started restocking the cooler.

When Jim sat at the table again, he raised his wine. "Maybe the day will come when you don't have to dig so deep."

The phone he had sat on the table beside his drink lit up with a text message. He glanced at it. "Uh oh. Looks like I'll have to sign off this evening." He saw me frown. "Sorry we have to cut the conversation short. I'm on call this week."

"On call?"

Pushing the half glass of wine in my direction, he said, "You're welcome to finish it. I've got a bit of a drive ahead."

"I thought you were retired."

"Yes. But I volunteer with a program through hospice called Last Watch. I sit with patients in their final hours when they are alone. Most have no friends or family." His eyes betrayed the sorrow behind his smile.

Awestruck, I tried to process how much compassion would be required to provide such a service—to sit patiently by and watch someone die.

"See you next week," he said and left.

When he was out the door, Jeff looked at me and asked, "What's up with Jim? Did you scare him off? He didn't even finish his wine."

* * *

On January 7th, David walked up to The Nook. He stopped on the street and stared suspiciously at the windows before coming up the steps and into the store. He moved deliberately through all the rooms, searching out anyone that might be lurking in some random corner before coming back to the front desk.

I waited, silently.

"Your mother," he said, and I stiffened. "I got a call."

It was a few seconds before I could choke out the word, "How?"

"Cancer."

"When?"

"Last week. New Year's Day." He turned to leave, but stopped at the door. "I thought you deserved to know."

I tried but could not speak the words *thank you*. Instead, I asked, "And what do you deserve, David?"

He stood another few seconds—his jaw clenching and releasing—and I thought I saw his head nod ever so slightly before he left.

My body went cold as I waited for the grief. But there was only anger— at my mother, David, my absent father. Even a certain self-loathing. Had she died alone—no family, no friends? Perhaps some stranger sat beside

163

her bed and soothed her with words of comfort that she would never have offered anyone else.

Jim had said he had a bit of a drive. Maybe it was he who sat by her side, stroking her hair, offering her assurances that, yes, she would meet her departed daughter soon.

I began to cry for all the wrong reasons.

* * *

Niki noticed the change in my personality over the next few days. She tried on more than one occasion to draw me out, but I couldn't explain any of it. A couple of light January snows slowed traffic in the store, so she let me sulk as long as I completed my tasks.

It had been two weeks, but Jim finally came in for his Saturday evening Merlot.

"How have you been?" he asked.

I poured myself a drink and followed him to a table. Before he could ask again, I preempted with my own question. "Your hospice patient?"

"He passed. Peacefully."

My shoulders relaxed when I heard *he*. At least is wasn't my mother.

"I can't believe you have the … fortitude to … to … ."

He reached his hand over to my arm. "It's not as hard as it would be if I knew them. Besides, I'd feel worse knowing they died alone."

"You're a gift to humanity," I said, feeling horridly inadequate.

"Oh, pshaw." His eyes squinted when he laughed. "Just doing the right thing."

"Someone has to," I mumbled and downed a large portion of the vodka.

"You still haven't answered my question," he said.

My mind jumped to his query about moving, and then I realized he meant my current state of health. "I'm good," I lied. To cover the obvious, I added, "It's been slow here, and I get bored easily."

We were interrupted by Casey and Jake coming over to say hello.

"Hey, you two," Casey said. "We didn't see either of you last weekend. How have you been?" There it was again, that social nicety that required one to gently pry into the affairs of another who didn't want to divulge too much.

She and Jim struck up a light conversation while I sat and listened. I realized then that my burdens were too heavy to share with Casey or Jim, or even Robbie who had become as close a friend as I had ever had—save Zoe. To the surprise of them all, I stood, said my goodnights and left.

Upstairs, in my apartment, the anemic light from a single floor lamp washed over the meager surroundings. On two walls, I had tacked seven of the latest drawings. Each had a missing part in the shape of a puzzle piece—each piece strategic in its placement. There were three more drawings to complete—two with similar omissions and one where all the missing pieces came together. The collection would not require the complex frames of the Mask series, but the works themselves did require a great deal of planning to be sure the assembled parts of the final drawing would be true to the original nine works and yet would fit together to form a new whole.

I worked all night on drawing number eight. When I had a good start, I set it aside and walked into the bathroom. In the mirror, I studied my face until I could stare past the paternal side of my genetic inheritance, until I could clearly see my mother. I reached into the drawer and pulled out a pair of scissors. Grabbing a lock of hair, I measured to my first knuckle and cut, repeating the process again and again.

When I'd finished, I stripped down and stepped into the steaming hot shower. I stood with my hands on either side of the nozzle and let the water rinse through my hair, run down my face, redden my skin. When the water began to cool on its own, I stepped out and dried off. At four in the morning, I slipped into bed.

* * *

When I walked into the shop on Tuesday, Niki's jaw dropped. "Becca! Your hair!"

I ran my fingers through the short spikes and gave a little nod.

"You okay? It's not … "

"No," I quickly assured her. "It's not chemo." I put my purse behind the desk and checked in. "I just felt like shaking things up a bit."

"Well, you've been so down lately, you had me worried. I will say, though, it's cute."

"Thanks. And sorry I've been in such a mood."

"Hey," she said, waving my concern away with a smile. "It happens."

All day long, the people who knew me would wander in and comment in surprise. Don, of course, thought it looked particularly unfeminine. Most of the women loved it. I worried, briefly, that Jim would find my new coif repugnant, but I remembered his strong feminist bent. If he found my shorn head repulsive, he would kindly keep it to himself. The one thing I had not prepared for was the tedium of reassuring everyone I was in good health. By the end of my shift, I had become untypically ill-tempered about their concern.

I excused myself and headed home. Outside the door to my apartment, a large package waited on the small rug that held my wet or muddy boots in winter. I unlocked the door and carried the box to the table. I ran a knife along the tape, releasing the flaps, and pulled a carefully-wrapped object from a sea of shredded newsprint. Taking my time, I surgically removed layer after layer of wrapping until, at last, I held in my hands a stunning piece of glass—a crown of delicate and brilliantly-colored fingers rising up from a clear crystal base. I pushed the box and wrappings to the floor and set the bowl center stage.

"Thank you," I whispered to my distant conspirator.

The work was complete. No one, not even Robbie, would be allowed to see the pieces intended for only one set of eyes. When the time was right, I would search out the proper way to display them. For now, they were stacked facing the wall, hiding their skeletons, waiting for the light of day.

On my trips to the library, I continued to search out news of Lena. Though her parents still pushed information out to the public, fewer and fewer outlets paid attention. Even the Internet memes—recycled, rehashed, falsified by a hundred attention-seeking drudges—dwindled. On occasion, her face would pop up with a different name, a different state, a different circumstance attached to it. I mourned not just her presumed death, but the corruption of her life brought on, in part, by my cowardice. Yet it was David's cruelty, magnified by the callousness of strangers, that was the real crime. In the dark hours alone in my apartment, I stared at the bowl and wept.

Chapter Thirteen

The Wednesday of spring break, I sorted overstock books for a display Niki had organized. Business was slow with the students gone. Lauren chose to stay in town and work extra hours, but Madi had opted for a road trip with friends. Through one of the students, I discovered that David would be prepping a new exhibit at the Holt-Russell gallery. I wondered if Parmenter Hall would be unlocked.

"Lauren, would you mind if I took some extra time at lunch to run an errand?"

She looked up from the computer and said, "Not at all. It's not like we're swamped."

I thanked her and made my way to campus. Inside Parmenter Hall, Louis, the security guard I'd met my first day on campus, nodded from behind his glass wall. The gallery doors ahead stood open, and I could see a number of crates and boxes around the floor. The pieces themselves had already been extracted, but lay in wait for the walls to be prepared for hanging. I walked into the room and began to study the photo-realistic oils of urban and rural landscapes.

Lovely, I thought, looking at the skill in execution, the composition, the artist's use of occasional pops of color in otherwise neutral settings. I could be as detailed with a pencil, but my watercolors were much more loose. I hadn't tried oils in years. I set that idea aside, and continued surveying each piece.

Halfway through the exhibit, I heard voices from the hall just before David and another man wandered in. David stopped, unsure what to do, and waited for me to say something. When I didn't, he directed the other man's attention my way.

"Russ, this is Becca …" he hesitated. "Mills, is it?"

When he introduced Russ, I nodded but kept silent.

The man walked over and firmly shook my hand. "Nice to meet you."

"The work is outstanding," I said. "Such incredible detail."

"Thanks. I'm really grateful to David for setting up this show." He looked around. "It's a great venue."

"Yes, a lovely gallery." We stood in a stalemate, each waiting for the other to speak. Before it became too awkward, I said my goodbyes and walked out, nodding once more at Louis as I passed.

Before I'd reached the bottom of the steps outside, David caught up to me and grabbed my arm.

"What are you playing at?" he asked, his eyes narrow.

I pulled my arm out of his grip and faced him directly.

"My life is my own," I said. "I will not let you dictate what I do with it. Never again."

"That still doesn't explain why you're here." He stepped back and looked around, making sure Russ had not followed. "I know it was you who phoned the Nebraska patrol." For a moment, he looked almost boyish. "I know you have reason to hate me."

He glanced at the scar on my forehead, wholly visible now that my hair no longer covered it. Reflexively, I ran my finger across it.

"Why not just turn me in?" he asked. "Come forward. Accuse me."

It was then that I understood why David had not yet exposed my identity even though he was now suspect in a second disappearance. As much as I refused to exonerate him by coming forward, he feared that I had some evidence beyond the scar to establish his guilt, something that would not only prove the assault, but his attempted cover up afterward. If that evidence existed, it would be impossible for him to shake the stigma a second time. Lena's vanishing was too coincidental. The publicity alone would ruin his career.

"I have my reasons," I finally said.

He looked genuinely wounded. "Lena. You think I hurt her, too." He brought his hands to his face and rubbed the stress from his eyes. "I did not touch her," he insisted. "I have no idea where she is."

Louis stepped out of Parmenter and headed down to his motorized cart in preparation for his security rounds. I took the opportunity to back away another step.

"There may come a day," I said, "when everyone knows the entire truth. Meanwhile, get used to the fact that I live here. I've made Baldwin my home. If we run into each other on occasion, I make no apologies for it."

"No apologies. Yet you don't seem to have any trouble making it happen."

"In a town the size of Baldwin? I live and work in a three-block area. It's no trouble at all." I should not have exposed myself so completely, but I no longer cared if he knew where I lived.

David turned away and disappeared into Parmenter. I returned to work and finished setting up the display on the discount shelves.

* * *

Our encounter in March seemed to break some of the tension between us. David passed by regularly again on his way to lunch with a colleague or a student or two. I couldn't help but note the students were almost always attractive young women. Old habits.

In a rare moment, a friend or coworker would invite David to The Nook for a drink. As often as he could, he would direct them to sit outside on the patio. If I was on duty, I stayed at the front desk—out of sight, but within earshot. Off duty, if I was already seated at one of the bar tables when he came in, I refused to give up my space in deference to him. He was invading *my* space, after all.

One afternoon, David and two students—giddy young women— came in for a drink. Don was in the middle of an introspective moment.

"My oldest sister, Betty Ruth, was the best one of us all," Don said, losing his genial smile. "She died, in November will be two years now. She was in the hospital." He raised his head and grinned at a memory. "She got up and she started to eat like maybe she was gonna be okay." His chin fell to his chest again. "But she died. Dammit to hell. Just one person outside of family showed up. I couldn't believe my oldest brother didn't show up for the wake." Don lowered his head. "Maybe he couldn't."

We all sat quietly, sobered by the moment. And then he laughed.

"She used to grab my ears," he said, reaching his fist out to grasp the air. "I told her, if I get big ears, it's all your fault!"

David glanced at me, condescension in his eyes for Don's demeanor. I glared back, trying to shame him for daring to judge.

He and his students ordered their drinks and took them outside.

Don let his eyes follow the trio out the door, and I could see his disdain for David's type—academia's elite that had never spent time in a world outside of higher education, sorely lacking real-world experience.

"Assholeo," Don mumbled, glancing at me.

"For sure," I said, nodding. "Don't let him intimidate you in the least. I would pit your character against his any day."

"Why, thank you," Don said, raising his glass. "Much appreciated."

I withdrew into a corner and watched the regulars fall into their rhythm.

There were things I wanted and things I needed. I wanted revenge, but I also wanted peace of mind. I needed justice for Lena, to hold David's feet to the fire. Part of me wanted to maintain my anonymity in Baldwin, while the greater part of me needed to reclaim my identity. Lena—whatever had happened to her—was the key to reconciling everything. David certainly would not volunteer that information. Not without provocation. That was my plan—to push him to the point of breaking.

* * *

The Lumberyard Arts Center hosted four art walks through the summer, each on the third Friday of the month. June through September, the artist openings coincided with activities and sidewalk art projects that brought out numbers larger than most other times of the year. Creatives vied for those months, hoping for better sales. In June, the artist featured in the gallery specialized in encaustic painting using hot wax to create works with three-dimensional textures. Outside the arts center, several artists set up displays on tables or easels. A bluegrass band performed from the pavilion in the park between the center and the post office—a large grassy area turned community playground.

It was my volunteer job to attend the refreshment table and helped pour wine. Most of the Open Art members wandered in through the evening. We visited or analyzed the art or talked over our own projects.

"You haven't shared your latest work with us," Susan was saying. "Why don't you hang one of your new pieces in the classrooms?"

"Soon. When are you going to have your own show?" I asked, diverting the conversation.

"Oh, never!" she said. "I couldn't put myself out there like this."

"You should reconsider," I told her. "Your work is beautiful."

She waved off the compliment. "I'm not brave enough."

Through the evening, I kept coming back to her words. She thought me brave. My Mask series had certainly laid bare my inner turmoil. But if I was truly brave, I would have put my real name on the work. That old cowardice still hung like a veil over my life.

CHAPTER FOURTEEN

Summer turned mercilessly hot. I had suffered the hundred-degree temperatures in Phoenix but never in this type of humidity. So often I had heard of the difference, but this was the first time I knew it to be true. Retreating to The Nook during the day helped, but the nights in the apartment still only cooled into the low nineties. By mid July, I begged my landlady to install one of the air conditioners.

"I'm surprised you've gotten by this long," she said as her husband inserted the unit in the kitchen window. She glanced at the minimal furniture and piles of art, but looked back at me without judgment. It was a studio space, after all. Not a rental for people of means.

"When it's just me, I can get by. I'm a summer person," I explained. "But I couldn't have a guest up here in this heat."

When her husband had plugged the unit into the outlet, he tested the controls. "Looks like it's working," he said. "It will take some time to catch up, though." To mark his words, he wiped the sweat from his forehead.

Before he left the kitchen, he glanced and pointed at the bowl on the table. "That's beautiful! Did you make it?"

"No. I bought it." I realized how incongruous the bowl looked in my spare apartment. In more ways than one, it was the most valuable possession I owned.

When they left, I showered and went to work.

Kenzie sat chatting with Don, drawing out his past.

"When I was a kid," he was saying, "I went to a psychiatrist. I had a little issue starting fires. He had my mom stay in the other room so he could talk to just me. We talked for a little while. Easy stuff. Then he started asking things I didn't want to answer. Finally, he said, 'Don, I don't have any idea why you start fires.'" He lowered his voice. "I didn't show him my back."

Kenzie's eyes widened.

Don was silent for a moment, that far-off look he would sometimes get in his eyes. "Then that psychiatrist told me, 'But you're smarter than any of the teachers in that school!' I didn't start a fire after that."

I sat contemplating how many times Don's life could have fallen down that rabbit hole sending him to prison—to oblivion. I wondered what in his character had kept steering him away from that darker part of himself. Neither David nor I had been tested so severely, and yet neither of us had passed through the crucible with our honor intact.

* * *

Two days later, I stood near the door of The Nook and watched a squirrel run along the handrail of the patio. On the opposite side of the street, David stood looking at the front of the building. He kept his eyes on the north window as he walked across High and hesitated at the sidewalk. Once he lost view of the window, he raced up the steps and into the store.

"Where is she?" he shouted while running to the north room. A few minutes later, he rushed back to where I stood. I slid a stack of books into place.

"Where's who?" I asked, turning to face him.

"Don't," he said, holding a hand up in warning. "I know she was here."

"I don't know who you're talking about. It's a slow day. I'm the only one who's been here for the last hour."

"Lena was standing in the window. I saw her!"

At that moment, a book from a shelf several feet away from either of us flung itself onto the floor. David jumped. Use to the paranormal events, I calmly walked over and picked it up.

He eyed me suspiciously. "Some kind of trick?"

"No trick," I promised. "Didn't you know? The store is haunted." I held the book up for him to see. "No strings."

Before I could react, David was in my face, his hand squeezing my upper arm. "No more games," he demanded. He grabbed the book from my hand and pitched it into the shelves, bringing down a full row of general fiction novels. He glared at me. "I might have to finish what I started." He pushed me back into the shelves and stormed out.

I recovered my balance and stared at the pile on the floor. On top laid *The Vanishing Half.* Was that the book that first fell? How ironic, I thought, but couldn't remember. Rubbing my arm, I walked to the north room and checked the storage area. The back door was locked. Everything else was in order.

The doorbell rang, and I walked back to the front room half expecting to see David again. But it was Jim. He stared at the mess and raised his eyebrows.

"You okay?"

"Fine," I assured him. I started picking up books and checking for damage. Those that could not go back as new I would pay for myself. They could still be sold as used.

"Need help?"

"Don't worry about it. Besides, what are you doing here mid-week? It's not Saturday or book club night."

"No." His eyes brightened. "I was in town for another reason and came to ask if you'd like to have dinner with me this evening."

"Oh," I said, pointing a shaming finger at him. "I'm an afterthought, am I?"

"Never." The banter between us had become quite comfortable. "I apologize that it's short notice."

I grabbed another few books and checked them over. "I wish I could," I said, "but I already have plans."

"A rain check then," he said, tipping his ball cap.

To his surprise, I stepped over and kissed him on the lips. "A rain check."

At five, I walked the block and a half to my apartment. Inside, I closed the door and rested against it.

"You were perfect," I said, acknowledging the woman in the chair.

Gena looked at the mark on my arm, red where David's fingers had pressed too hard.

I nodded. "Yes, he was furious."

She rose up from the chair and came to stand near me. "Did he threaten you?"

"I expected he would. We're pressing all the right buttons."

She removed the blonde wig and tossed it near her overnight case. From inside her pocket, she pulled a key and handed it to me. "It was close. I didn't think I'd get the back door locked in time."

"I'm glad you did," I said, putting the key back in my purse.

* * *

I did not imagine David would set foot in the shop again, but just in case, Gena and I agreed to stay in touch. University classes would start again in a month. I knew what I wanted to do, I just wasn't sure I could pull it off without help. Over the two years I'd been in Baldwin, I had been networking, building relationships—some intentional, some accidental. One, in particular, would be very useful in the next couple of weeks.

Two days before the start of Baker's semester, Lauren—wide-eyed and excited—hurried into The Nook. She walked to the bar tables where Niki and I were working on publishing projects and book orders.

"Oh my god," she began. "Did you guys hear what just happened at Baker?"

I tempered my interest, but Niki played into Lauren's excitement.

"So, it seems that someone—no one knows exactly who—found a way into the Holt Russell gallery at Parmenter Hall and hung an unauthorized show. Like, how does that happen?"

"What?" Niki asked. "Isn't there security?"

"Yeah, there is. That's what has them all weirded out. Nobody knows when it happened or how they got in."

"No security cameras?"

Lauren popped her backpack on another table and sat down. "You would think," she said, "but I haven't heard."

The Holt-Russell gallery, empty through the summer, had been easy to access with Louis's help. Late night, on the Tuesday before, I had walked the ten pieces of art across campus and met him on the west side of the building—the basement door.

I felt only slightly ashamed of the excuse I had given him as we took the pieces up the stairs and into the gallery.

"You can leave," I had told him. "I can let myself out."

Louis had taken a cursory glance at the art and left.

For twenty minutes, I had worked in the semi-dark, the light of the streetlamps seeping in through the windows. The drawings were frameless, so I had tacked them to the wall with push pins. Gena had supplied the reference photos. I supplied the layers of meaning.

Each unsigned work showed an aspect of Lena's life from junior high through her move to Baldwin. She was always smiling. Engaged in life. The puzzle shapes omitted from each work came together in the tenth drawing. The contours within the shapes—obviously lifted from the other nine—spelled out Where is she?

My curiosity got the best of me. "So, what happened? To the exhibit?"

"That's the crazy thing," Lauren said, grinning large. "The art professor, Sante, he saw it and went berserk! I guess security walked in on him ripping the drawings down and shredding them into bits."

"Whoa!" Niki said, her eyes wide.

"Yeah, who does that?"

Timidly, I asked, "What were the drawings of?"

Lauren shrugged. "I heard they were portraits. They apparently set him off. Big time!"

I didn't know whether to laugh or cry. My work—my hours of planning and the painstaking detail I had executed to pull off my stunt—had been trashed. The exhibit was valid in its own right, I felt. The work was good. Yet the torment inflicted had to be worth the loss. Still, I had not expected David to react so rashly.

"Did he get fired?" Niki asked.

"Oh, yeah!" Lauren laughed. "They've been interviewing students to find out who the work belonged to, but nobody knows."

David had to know—not only because of the subject, but he now knew my style.

Lauren's news brought me no satisfaction. I sat considering the consequences and realized that, despite David's reaction, we were no closer to finding Lena. I stewed over what might happen to the students who were now left without a professor for the fall semester. But finding Lena had to be worth the turmoil. This justice had to be served.

"I'm not feeling well," I told Niki, suddenly anxious.

She gave me a sympathetic look and said, "You can go home, if you want. There's nothing crucial."

I thanked her and left for my apartment.

Upstairs, I poured a glass of ice water and sat at the kitchen table. My finger traced the many oscillations of the glass bowl as I considered where my life was headed. I had succeeded, finally, in turning David's life upside down—something that should have happened seven years earlier. But my own circumstance had improved very little. I was still a ghost in many respects.

Caught up in my own thoughts, I did not hear the footsteps climbing the stairs until they hit the landing and turned toward my apartment. After two years, I knew, almost by instinct, the footsteps of the other two tenants. No one else should have known the combination to the downstairs lock. I jumped when someone knocked.

"Who is it?" I leaned around to see a fuzzy silhouette on the other side of the textured glass insert in the door.

There was no answer. Only the pounding of a fist.

Stepping into the living space, I asked again. "Who is it?"

There was an explosion of glass as the tempered window glazing crumbled into the room. I ducked, raising my hands to protect my face. When I looked up again, David was reaching through the opening, searching for the lock.

"Stop!" I yelled, but he twisted the latch and pushed the door open.

He stepped into the room, and immediately was caught off guard by how spartan it was. "This?" he said, laughing. "This is what you've ruined me for?"

"Are you mad? You think this is about me?"

"Isn't it?" he asked as he walked over to the stack of frames facing the wall.

"David," I choked, incredulous. "You assaulted me! You buried me alive!" I could not speak the words I wanted to—that it was I who had paid the penance for his misdeeds. That burden was my own.

"And what about Lena?" I finally asked.

His eyes flared. "What about her?"

His callous tone—his dismissal—sent me into a rage. I ran at him, beating his chest with both fists. He caught my wrists and wrestled me onto the bed.

"You fool!" he shouted. He twisted my arms together and grasp them in one hand, and then yanked me to my feet. "The two of you have been conjuring this plot to get back at me."

I strained against his grip. "Two of us? Lena's been missing for months now."

"Let her go," said a voice from behind.

We both twisted to see Gena standing in the doorway. Before David could react, she was on his back, her arms wrapped around his neck, choking him. He fell back, letting go of my wrists. He managed to pull Gena off of him and push her to the floor. His hands wrapped tightly around her neck.

I could run for help, but I knew she wouldn't survive his grip for long. On instinct, I grabbed the bowl from the kitchen table and struck David in the head. He fell to one side, disoriented. Terrified of what I'd done, I let the bowl slip from my hands, crash to the floor. Shatter.

"Becca," Gena said. "He needs to be punished."

I dropped to the floor and grabbed David's legs to hold them steady. "We should tie him up."

Gena reached for a shard of glass laying near David's head. As he began to stir, she pushed the razor-edged finger of glass into the side of his neck.

David opened his eyes and looked at her, and then me. He started to sit up, but felt the sting at his throat as a small slice drew a drop of blood. He stared up at Gena with pure hatred in his eyes.

"Why are you doing this to me?"

"To *you*?" she shrieked. "You heartless son-of-a-bitch!"

"You don't think her sister deserves justice?" I asked, trying to steady my voice.

David's disdain turned to me. "What do you mean her sister? Lena has no sister."

My eyes turned to Gena's twisted grin, and the pit of my stomach churned.

"David always told me you were a fool," she said. "You truly are."

My face chilled as the blood ran from it. "Lena?" My thoughts scrambled in a hundred different directions. I released my grip on David's legs and crawled back against the wall. I had been played. Again.

I stared at the two of them—Lena pressing her makeshift dagger deeper into his flesh, David daring her with his eyes.

"Lena," I said, regaining my composure. "Don't."

She glared at me. "He deserves it! You know he does."

"And what do you deserve?" I asked.

Her eyes watered as her hand gripped the finger of glass tighter, pressed it deeper—a trickle of blood running down David's neck.

I stood and walked to her side. "Don't," I said again.

As I reached for her shoulders, David struggled to push her hand away. She lunged at him just as I wrapped my arms around her waist, pulling her back. We fell to the floor, and Lena began to sob.

We're sitting at The Nook tonight and listening to Don complain about retirement.

"Man, I'm kinda stressed. Don't know what I'll do without a shop, and I can't afford the equipment. I'll miss it, for sure."

The party was Kinzie's idea. She bought banners, made treats. Niki made dip. There are cookies and queso. Don is trying not to tear up as he makes the rounds.

"Maybe I'll take a train trip just for fun," he says. "Something through the mountains."

I look at Jim sitting across from me. "I'm ready to answer that question."

It takes a moment before he nods. "And?"

"I opened a bank account. Would you like to help me pick out new furniture?"

"I'd be honored," he says.

I think about Jim and wonder sometimes. But I'm not ready. Physically, perhaps, but emotionally I'm still a newborn. Still learning what I want for my own life unencumbered by the expectations of others. My eyes wander around the bar at the collection of personalities I now consider my surrogate family. When I look back at Jim, he raises his glass.

"To friends, then?"

"For now," I say. "To friends."